WHEN THE DEVIL
CAME TO ENDLESS

WHEN THE DEVIL CAME TO ENDLESS

•

CHARLES BOECKMAN

AVALON BOOKS
THOMAS BOUREGY AND COMPANY, INC.
401 LAFAYETTE STREET
NEW YORK, NEW YORK 10003

© Copyright 1996 by Charles Boeckman
Library of Congress Catalog Card Number: 95-96224
ISBN 0-8034-9171-9

PRINTED IN THE UNITED STATES OF AMERICA
ON ACID-FREE PAPER
BY HADDON CRAFTSMEN, SCRANTON, PENNSYLVANIA

To Talmadge Powell, mentor and life-long friend,
who helped launch this writer's career.

Chapter One

The tornado struck Endless, Texas, at 3:30 in the afternoon of Friday, September 29, 1889. They say it was the worst tornado that ever hit Texas. They say it rained for four solid days after the tornado smashed the town.

Of the fifteen hundred people living in the town, a hundred and fifty were killed. Another four hundred were injured. The tornado cut a mile-wide swath, destroying or damaging most of the buildings in the town. And when it was over, a stick figure of a man sat atop a pile of rubble, playing his fiddle.

The day of the tornado, the stage bound for San Antonio left Endless at 3:00 P.M. Driving the team was Al Sanders, and riding shotgun beside him was Eddie Magan. Sheets of rain falling from a black sky popped against their slick-

1

ers and stung their faces. They sat with their heads bowed against the pelting rain. Gusts of wind buffeted the coach.

In the coach rode four people: Lorraine Crader, a widow, age forty, on her way to visit her niece in San Antonio; George Lowell, barbed-wire salesman; Ned Saxet, deputy sheriff; and Link Houston, his prisoner. Link was handcuffed.

There was little conversation in the stagecoach. The widow was looking nervously out of a window, uttering muffled gasps of anxiety with each gust of wind that shook the coach. She was filled with misgivings about starting out in this kind of weather. But her favorite niece in San Antonio was getting married that weekend. She couldn't bear to miss the wedding. It had taken her months to make the wedding gifts—a crocheted tablecloth and patchwork quilt. She only hoped they would be safe in her trunk on top of the coach. The driver had covered the luggage with a tarp and had assured her the baggage would stay dry. As strong as the wind had gotten, though, she worried that the tarp might blow off.

Beside her, the barbed-wire drummer took a flask from his coat pocket and, ignoring the disapproving look he got from the widow, had a long pull of bourbon. The old woman with her whimpering and exclamations of fright was getting on his nerves more than the lousy weather. He then lit a cigar which drew another scowl from the widow. Well, to hell with her. He wasn't going to let her spoil his good mood. He'd racked up a lot of sales this trip. When he collected his commission from the home office in San

Antonio, he was going to treat himself to a bath and a room at the St. Anthony Hotel. Later, he'd go to the Buckhorn Saloon for some serious drinking and maybe eat some tamales in the Mexican section of town. He could put up with a couple of days of bad weather and rough stagecoach travel for that.

He looked at the two men facing him, one wearing a badge, the other obviously his prisoner. He thought he sure wouldn't want to be in that poor devil's shoes, headed for a long stretch behind bars. The prisoner looked like a fairly clean-cut young fellow in his mid twenties. Couldn't always tell from outward appearances, though. The kid might be a professional gunslinger. He shivered at the thought of spending years of his life cooped up in a cramped cell. The thought was so depressing, he had to console himself with another pull at his flask.

This was not a trip that Deputy Sheriff Ned Saxet relished. He did not like giving up the soft arms of the black-eyed beauty, Maria Alvarez. Maria was the youngest in a family of four brothers and six sisters. Old Alvarez, her father, worked at the stables when he wasn't drunk. Maria took in washing and did odd cleaning jobs around town. She swept out the town jail and sheriff's office every day and cooked food for the prisoners. That was how Saxet had met her. Life for him at this point was good. He hated leaving Maria even for the week it would take to transport young Link Houston to the state pen in Huntsville and return. He hated the uncomfortable two-day stagecoach trip from the West Texas town of Endless to San Antonio. From there, at least they could make railroad connections to Houston and Huntsville. Still, it added up to a week when he'd rather be doing other things.

Why didn't they just hang the kid and be done with it? Everybody believed he'd killed Albert Milam. He'd fought with Milam and threatened him earlier the day of the killing. Walt Sawyer swore he heard a shot and saw Link Houston leave Milam's office the night he was murdered.

Circumstantial evidence. That's what Link's lawyer told the jury. Saxet was surprised that the court-appointed lawyer, old senile Victor Crenshaw, even knew what the term meant. "Circumstantial evidence," the drooling, palsied old coot had mumbled to the jury. Nobody actually saw Link do the shooting. And everybody on the jury had to admit that Walt Sawyer, the town drunk, was not the most reliable witness in the world.

Still, Link Houston was known to be a hot-tempered young man who had been in more than one fight and had threatened Milam. When Link found out he was wanted for the murder of Albert Milam, he had tried to run away. Sheriff Matt Blake had to bring him back to stand trial. That was a pretty good admission of guilt, wasn't it?

The upshot had been that the jury came in with a guilty verdict, but they couldn't quite bring themselves to hang Link. Instead of finding him guilty of murder with malice aforethought, which would have got him hung in short order, the jury found him guilty of a lesser charge of voluntary manslaughter, which shocked everyone in town. There ought to be a hanging, it was generally agreed.

The judge, not happy with the verdict, gave Link a stiff sentence of fifteen years at hard labor in Huntsville which, in that hellhole, was as good as a life sentence. If by some miracle, Link was still alive at the end of that time, he'd be a broken old man.

Sitting beside the deputy, Link Houston was staring out of the stagecoach window, his mood as dark as the weather outside, his morale at an all-time low. His future was without hope.

He hadn't killed Milam, much as he'd wanted to. He was miles away at the time, in a poker game at a little town on the border. Unfortunately, the game had been with strangers, cowboys driving a herd of beef up to Kansas. There was no way he could find them to provide him with an alibi. And he'd lost the poker game. His usual run of bad luck.

It was another case of bad luck that had brought him back to Endless a few months ago. Actually, it was a knife stuck in his guts that brought him back. There was no place else for him to go. He'd gone busted in the game that started the knife fight. He'd lost both the game and the knife fight. The quack who passed for a doctor in the town where it happened poured whiskey in the wound, sewed him up, then told him he was probably going to die in a week or two from blood poisoning if he didn't bleed to death internally before that.

Some kind of homing instinct brought him back to Endless and his father's ranch to die. He knew he wasn't entirely welcome there. But when he rode into the yard and fell out of the saddle with his shirt and pants soaked with blood, his father had to let him stay.

He didn't exactly get the traditional prodigal son's welcome home.

Life had not been easy for his father, Ben Houston. Ben had been in the wave of gray that Pickett led across the open field to the Union lines on Cemetery Ridge at Gettysburg in '63. He lost his right arm in that futile charge. He lost more than that. It wouldn't have been so bad, losing an arm and most of his friends, if it hadn't all turned out to be futile. He could never accept that defeat. He had never accepted the Union's offer of amnesty.

Life hadn't treated Ben much better after he came home from the war. His wife left him. Link, his only son, had turned out to be a disappointment. Link had a rebellious, reckless streak that got him in one scrape after another. He could never face the tough realities of life like getting some schooling or sticking to an honest job. When a situation got tough for him, he just ran away.

When he was a little tyke, Link had brought some pleasure to Ben's life. The times Ben liked to remember were going fishing and hunting with the boy, teaching him to ride a horse. They'd been close for those few years back then. Link had been a cute, tousle-haired youngster. Maybe that was his trouble. He'd gotten by on his good looks and his way of charming people. He'd never entirely grown up. Inside, he was still the kid with the angelic smile that folks made a fuss over.

As Link grew older, he and Ben became strangers. Ben

got tired of bailing the kid out of trouble. Link had gambling fever; he couldn't stay away from the cards. Ben paid off his gambling debts, paid his fines for getting in fights. Finally, Ben got fed up and told Link to straighten up or get out. Link said he was never cut out to be a rancher, saddled his horse and rode away to lead his own life. That was seven years ago, when Link was eighteen. Occasionally, when he was in the area, he'd stop by the ranch for a brief visit. It was always a strained affair, and he wondered why he'd come back.

This time, he passed out when he rode into the yard. When his vision came swimming back, he was on a cot. His father was pressing a blood-soaked towel hard against his belly to stop the hemorrhaging.

"I'm going to die, Ben," he mumbled. "Doctor said I'll die in a week or so."

"Bull," Ben growled. "I know a few things about stab wounds. Saw plenty of them at Shiloh, Chancelorsville, Gettysburg. This ain't no fatal wound. You ain't gonna die. It would probably be good riddance, but you're too ornery and worthless to die."

Sure enough, his father, the old Reb soldier who'd fought under Lee, knew more than the quack doctor. The pain was god-awful. He clamped his teeth on his lip to keep from howling. He sweated from fever. But he lived. In a week, Link was sitting up in bed. In ten days, he was tottering around the room. Ben fed him steaks and fresh vegetables from his garden. In a month, Link had regained his full strength and was able to ride into town for a game of poker.

The relationship between him and his father changed a little after that month. Some of the old wounds between them healed along with his body. Link knew his father had saved his life.

That didn't mean Link had mended his ways, and the chasm between them remained wide. But there was an unspoken truce, a kind of accepting of each other as individuals. Ben allowed Link to live at the ranch for a while.

It was at the saloon in town during a card game that Link heard about Ben's trouble with the bank. That night, at the farm, Link had chided Ben for not telling him about it. Ben just shrugged. He wasn't the kind to talk about his personal problems.

"How bad is it?" Link had asked.

"Bad enough, I guess," Ben muttered.

Link noticed that Ben had several drinks of whiskey before supper and more during the meal. That wasn't like Ben.

"They're saying in town that you might lose this place."

"A man can't keep his business private in this town," Ben growled.

Link gave his father a troubled look. This land had been in the family for three generations. "What happened?"

His father shrugged. "Run of bad luck. The drought we've had for three years. Lost a lot of my cattle. What I have left is so poorly that I couldn't get beans for them. I had to borrow money to see me through until we get rain and I can build the herd back up. I took out the loan with the understanding that the bank would carry me until things picked up. They know I'm good for it. Trouble is, Albert Milam, who has taken over as bank president, has had his eye on this place for a long time. If he could get this place and the Sanchez land south of me, he'd have access to the river. The Sanchez family has agreed to sell their place. He's tried to buy this place from me, but I wouldn't sell. Now, unless we get rain soon and I can fatten up some beef to sell, he's going to get this place anyway."

"But you said he'd agreed to carry the loan until things picked up for you."

"He's doing that for all the other ranchers around here," Ben said bitterly. "But he isn't lusting after their land the way he is mine."

"Don't you have some kind of paper that says they'll carry you like they promised?"

Ben said, "I took out the loan when Mack Linden was president of the bank. I signed the regular loan note. Mack told me that was just a bank formality, but he wouldn't call in the loan until the drought was over and I got my herd back in shape. We shook hands on the deal. Mack and I knew each other all our lives. With Mack Linden a handshake was as good as any legal paper a San Antonio lawyer could draw up. Trouble is, Mack dropped dead of a heart attack a few months ago. Sid Milam who owns the bank put his brother, Albert, in charge. Tough luck for me. Albert's calling in the loan when it comes due this fall. No way I can raise the money by then."

"Can you go to Sid Milam?"

Ben snorted. "Heck'uva lot that would do. You know

Sid. The man's got a heart of stone. He don't care nothin' about a small rancher like me. We never had any use for each other. He never liked me 'cause I was a Johnny Reb. He was one of them carpetbaggers that come down here after the war. Didn't have a pot to his name when he got off the stage twenty years ago. Went to grabbing land from widows whose men got killed in the war. Now he owns most of the land around here, includin' the town and the bank.''

Link worried about his father's situation, but there wasn't much he could do about it. He turned to the only way he knew to make money—cards. If he had a run of good luck, maybe he could raise the funds to pay off the debt.

Then he met Laura Sontag, the daughter of Elijah Sontag, the preacher, and life for Link Houston took on a whole new dimension. Until that point in his life, the females he had known were mostly saloon women. Laura was like a pure angel. From the first time he laid eyes on her, he knew he loved her. It wasn't easy for them to get together. Her father knew all about Link's reputation. He considered Link to be a worthless card-playing sinner bound straight for hell. He forbade Laura to go anywhere near Link. The times they were together were stolen moments, but all the sweeter for it.

If his luck had been good he would have hit a big poker pot and paid off his father's bank loan. Then he would have settled down to helping Ben run the ranch. He would have proven to his father and Laura's father that he'd mended his ways, and he would have married Laura.

That's the way it would end in a storybook. What happened in real life is that he didn't win the card games. And he got in a fight with Albert Milam over the bank loan. That night Milam was murdered. When Link heard the sheriff was going to arrest him for the murder, he had reacted in his customary way: he'd panicked and tried to run away. And now he was on his way to Huntsville and he'd never see Laura again.

Somewhere in Endless was the person who shot Albert Milam to death, walking around free as the air, while Link would spend his days in a miserable cell. The sheriff was so convinced that Link was the murderer, he hadn't even bothered to find out if maybe somebody else committed the crime. He just threw Link in jail and announced that the murder was solved.

Link looked out at the weather that seemed to be getting worse. Clouds were being torn and whipped across the dark sky. Rain swirled around the coach and turned the road into muddy ruts that forced the team to work hard. Another cruel joke of fate. The rain was ending the drought, but it was coming too late for his father to save his land.

Link saw mesquite and huisache branches whipping around like arms of tortured beings in hell. As bad as it was, he wanted to remember all of it, this rugged, open land of West Texas that he was never going to see again.

Up on the driver's seat, Al Sanders snapped his long whip, urging the team to work harder at pulling the coach along the soggy road. At this rate, it was going to take more than two days to get to San Antonio.

Beside him, Eddie Magan tried to pull his slicker tighter. Cold rainwater was running from the brim of his hat. Some of it had gotten under the collar of his slicker and was trickling down his back. He was wet and uncomfortable. He groped for his tobacco in a pocket, took a large bite, and chewed it into a sweet, liquid mass. It gave him some measure of comfort. When his mouth was full, he leaned as far over as possible to send a stream of tobacco juice away from himself. The wind caught it and splattered it over the windows of the coach. He chuckled at what the passengers thought about that.

That was when he became aware of a curious, distant roaring sound. It reminded him a little of a freight train coming at them. There was no sense in that, of course, there being no rails out in this godforsaken corner of Texas. Nothing here but scrubby mesquite, cactus, buzzards, lizards, rattlesnakes, and the few people with no better sense than to live here. He was from New Orleans. Civilization. How life's circumstances had landed him here, riding shotgun on a dinky stagecoach line was something that evaded him. He had never seemed to have much control over his life. The winds of chance had blown him every which way. Too much liquor, getting messed up with the wrong woman, a knife fight at a card game that left one man dead . . . so he'd wound up sitting here on this bouncing seat, wet and cold, dreaming of the time he could save enough money to get back to New Orleans and civilization. It was a dream that kept slipping through his fingers the way the money did. Whenever payday came around, he'd get a bath and a shave and stop by a saloon for a drink. Just one, he'd tell himself, to get the taste of prairie dust he'd been eating all week out of his mouth. Two days later, he'd wake up in some stinking border town, stone broke with nothing to show for the weekend but a blasting headache. It was a pattern he hadn't been able to break. But he would, he promised himself. He'd start saving his payday money and get back to New Orleans. And civilization.

The roaring was getting louder. His head had been bowed against the wind and rain. All he could see from below the wide rim of his hat was water running down from the brim and the flanks of the team heaving and struggling through the mud. But the sound made him look up. He got a splash of rain directly in his face. He wasn't aware of that. The sight that met his eyes drove everything else from his mind.

He uttered a gasped exclamation.

His eyes bulged. He yelled at Sanders, jabbing him frantically in the ribs and pointing at the thing in the sky. It was like something alive, an enormous funnel-shaped black thing with a great black tail reaching down from the sky, licking at the countryside as it came toward them like a black monster straight out of hell.

Sanders's body stiffened. "Oh, no!" he cried. "It's a twister, sure enough!"

"What's a twister?" Magan screeched.

"I ain't never seen one, but I've heard tell of them," Sanders yelled over the roar that was getting louder by the minute. Normally a considerate man who cared for his animals, he now lashed the team unmercifully.

It was useless. The juggernaut came straight at them. As it drew closer, Magan's bulging eyes saw dirt and branches and whole uprooted trees swirling around in the funnel. Then he saw something that turned his blood to ice water. He saw a big, longhorn steer being tossed around like a toy inside the funnel a hundred feet above the ground.

That was when he knew he was going to die.

Seconds before it hit, there was pandemonium inside the coach. The widow Crader gave a single, unearthly, piercing scream. The barbed-wire salesman who was taking a frantic gulp from his flask turned white as a sheet and spilled liquor all over his shirt front. Deputy Ned Saxet uttered a gasping curse. Link went tense, bracing himself, all thoughts of his personal trouble blanked from his mind.

The licking tail of the monster thing came on them, ripping great clumps of mesquite trees and cactus into its maw. It was a great, hungry beast devouring everything in its path. It took only seconds to splinter the stagecoach into matchsticks, gobbling it up and spitting wheels, luggage, framework into the next county.

Horses and human bodies became rag dolls. Some were picked up high into the sky, then thrown into the mud miles away. Some were impaled on broken tree stumps. Some were rolled over the ground and smashed into boulders.

Then the black funnel moved on, heading directly for the town of Endless.

Consciousness came back to Link in a dizzying wave.

He sat up, groaning. He didn't know where he was or what had happened. He was numb all over. His mind was dazed.

Gradually the numbness faded. In its place came pain all over his bruised body. The pain cleared the fog from his befuddled mind. He looked around, seeing a clearing a mile wide cut through the prairie chaparral. Slowly, his mind began functioning. Thought processes groped through the haze. Scraps of memory flashed by. He could remember riding in the stagecoach. The storm outside. That last moment when he glanced outside, heard the screams and cries around him, saw the black monster swooping out of the sky toward them, heard the ear-shattering roar.

Now he was sitting here on the wet ground, rain pouring down on him. He wiped his left hand across his eyes, trying to clear his vision. He didn't see the stagecoach anywhere. It had simply vanished. There were bits and pieces lying around. A wheel. The wagon tongue. One of the horses was sprawled out on the road, its neck and legs broken. Some of the luggage was scattered about. Pieces of clothing fluttered from broken mesquite stumps. One bundle of clothing looked different. It was on the other side of the road. Link stared at it. Then he realized it was the body of the widow. Her dead eyes were staring up at the sky. Rain splattered down on her white face.

Slowly realization filtered into his shocked mind. They had been struck by a cyclone, a tornado.

The next thing that came to Link's awareness was the pull of the handcuff on his right wrist. He looked at it and almost gagged. He was still handcuffed to the deputy. What was left of the deputy. Most of the clothing had been ripped from his body. His bare chest was white except where jagged, bloody edges of ribs poked through the skin. A splinter of wood had been driven like a spike into one eye, through his brain. The other bulging eye stared at Link with an expression of surprise. A puddle of blood had formed under his head and ran into the road in a small rivulet.

Link asked, how could it be that he survived while the storm had mangled the deputy who was sitting beside him? He remembered stories he'd heard about tornadoes—the freak pranks they played. A house blown to bits while the shed beside it was left untouched. A baby grabbed from its crib and left in a treetop, crying but unharmed. It was as if the storm were a live monster with a grotesque sense of humor. That's what some Indian cultures believed. An Indian once told Link that the old men in his tribe spoke of a legend—that the tornado was a creature who lived inside the earth. From time to time it became hungry, escaped out from a hole in the earth, and ate everything in its path.

Link stared at the handcuff still secured to the dead man's wrist. He fought off revulsion and worked his way down where he could reach Saxet's trousers. He groped through the wet, soggy cloth until he found the keys in a pocket. Quickly, he unlocked the handcuff from his wrist. The deputy's pistol and gun belt were tangled up in the trousers around the man's ankles. Link got the belt unbuckled, fastened it around his waist, and shoved the .45 Colt in the holster. Then he crawled quickly away, needing to distance himself from the broken body.

He got to his knees, then to his feet. It was at that point that the pain in his left leg hit him. When he put his weight on the leg, he cried out. The pain was excruciating. His vision swam for a moment, then came into focus. The agony made him weak and shaky.

He collapsed into a sitting position. He pulled up the left leg of his jeans. The pain was coming from below his knee, from somewhere above his ankle. He was almost certain his leg was broken, but he couldn't examine that part of his lower leg without removing his boot. As bad as the pain was, tugging at the boot to pull it off was out of the question.

He sat there for a moment, looking around. There was not a sign of life anywhere. He had seen the bodies of the widow and the deputy. He couldn't see anything of the others. As far as he could tell, he was the only person in the coach who had survived.

The full meaning of the situation hit him with a jolt. He was battered and bruised and probably had a broken leg, but he was alive. The Mexican border was fifty miles away to the southwest. Fifty miles and freedom. A new life, a fresh start, waited for him down there.

The awful roar of the tornado was moving away from this area. Link turned around. He saw the funnel in the sky as black and fearsome as ever, going in an eastern direction, headed straight for Endless. It would strike the town in a few minutes.

His blood ran cold. He stared at the beast in the sky, thinking of the terrible fate waiting the people of Endless.

Laura. His father. They could be badly hurt or killed. They would need help.

He sat, shivering in the soaking rain. An instinct of self-preservation urged him to save his own hide, to head southwest to the Mexican border as fast as he could. It was his usual pattern . . . running away from trouble.

But there was the thought of Laura in that awful storm. How could he run away to Mexico not knowing if she was dead or alive, if she was lying hurt in the rain and the mud, needing help?

He thought about his father too. His ranch was in the direct path of the tornado.

He'd be a fool, going back to Endless. If the law caught up with him, he'd get himself hung or be on his way to Huntsville again. But there was bound to be destruction and confusion following the storm. Possibly, he could slip into the town unnoticed. If Laura was all right, she might agree to run away to Mexico with him.

Maybe he'd be a fool to go back to Endless. But trying to limp across fifty miles of Texas prairie with a broken leg and no food or water was not a brilliant idea, either. He needed horses and food.

Looking around at the shattered tree branches on the muddy ground, he spied one that could serve as a crutch. He crawled to it, pulled himself to a standing position, keeping the weight off his injured leg.

He fitted the forked end of the branch under his left arm and began limping across the muddy, storm-stripped fields, following the tornado to the town of Endless.

Chapter Two

Laura Sontag huddled under the tarp she had pulled over her head for protection against the increasing storm. She urged Billy to a faster gait, slapping the reins against his flank. The horse was doing his best at pulling the wagon over the muddy road. There was a strange roaring sound in the air. The black, funnel-shaped cloud was moving fast in this direction.

Laura wasn't aware of the approaching tornado. She wasn't concerned about getting wet from the rain or killed by the storm. She didn't care about her own safety. If it weren't for her brother and sister, Paul and Ruth, home alone and no doubt frightened out of their wits, she wouldn't care if a bolt of lightning killed her right here and now. Her life had ended when she'd watched the stage-

coach taking Link away to prison. Inside, she had died. It
hurt bad that she couldn't at least go to his side, to let him
know what was in her heart, to give him what little comfort
she could. But she knew her father would find out. He had
strictly forbidden her to talk to Link.

"That young man is a wild one, headed for trouble,"
Elijah had said with a worried frown when it first became
known that Link had returned to Endless. When Link was
charged with the murder of Albert Milam, it had confirmed
Elijah's prediction. He thought he had done the right thing
in ordering Laura to have nothing to do with him.

Laura was a good girl. Never in her seventeen years had
she disobeyed her father until Link came into her life. Their
first meeting took place several weeks ago at Altman Brothers General Store. Laura was doing the week's shopping
for the family, carefully stretching the two dollars her father
had given her. The Sunday collection had been slim, and
this was going to be one of the weeks when they'd have
to get by on pinto beans and biscuits.

The Altman brothers, Jeff and Cave, had started out sell-
ing merchandise from steamboats up and down the Rio
Grande. Fifteen years ago, they had opened a small store
in Endless. They drew trade from ranchers, cowboys on
cattle drives, and lately from sod busters—German farm-
ers—who had begun settling in the area. The store had
prospered.

In the store's dim, crowded interior could be found almost every kind of human need, from kerosene to calico
to croup medicine. On the shelves were home remedies

such as castor oil and Epsom salts, writing slates and *McGuffey's Readers* for schoolchildren, plows, saddles, bridles, blankets, hats, and guns. Counters were piled high with grocery staples and dry goods. From the store's rafters hung cooking pots, hams, and slabs of bacon. Crowded around the floor were kegs of sugar, flour, and molasses. Smells of saddle leather, fresh-ground coffee, tobacco, pickled fish, and vinegar filled the air.

In the center of the store near a cracker barrel was a potbellied stove, a social gathering place where men sat and whittled and spat tobacco juice and talked about the weather and argued politics.

Laura paused at the counter that held frilly bonnets, sewing patterns, bolts of calicoes and muslins and ready-to-wear dresses. With all the chores waiting back home, she had no business wasting time there, daydreaming over things she couldn't possibly buy. It was probably sinful even thinking of such things. But she couldn't resist the attraction.

Today, a bolt of red fabric had caught her eyes. She paused to feel the silky material, imagining the kind of dress she could make for herself out of it. Not that such an impossible thing would ever happen. Material like this cost more than they'd have in a year. And even if her father had that kind of money, she could imagine his reaction to her showing up at the Sunday service in a red dress. She suppressed a giggle at the thought.

"That would look mighty pretty on you, Ma'am," a masculine voice drawled.

She looked up, startled, and saw a tall stranger leaning against a glass counter, looking at her with an amused expression. She had never seen him around Endless before. He looked to be in his mid twenties. He was nice looking, tall, slender. When he removed his hat to give her a polite bow, she saw that he had rich, curly light brown hair. What she noticed most about him were his soft brown eyes and the easy way he smiled.

He pushed himself away from the counter and ambled over in a lazy, strolling way to where she was standing. He held an end of the red fabric up beside Laura's cheek. ''Yes, Ma'am, with that gold hair of yours and those deep blue eyes, this color would look awful good on you.''

Laura felt her face grow hot and red. She was completely tongue-tied. It was the first time in her life a man had come up to her and talked in such a teasing, flirty way. She reckoned she ought to be insulted or mad or something, but she didn't feel any of those things. She was just hypnotized by those soft, brown laughing eyes.

She finally got her wits about her and hurried over to the store's main counter. Jeff Altman's wife standing behind the cash register was giving her a thin-lipped, disapproving look. Laura sure hoped that the stranger talking to her that way wouldn't start a round of gossip. She shuddered to think what her father would do if he heard about it.

She quickly took out her handkerchief in which the two dollars was tied, undid the knot and paid Mrs. Altman for the bags of flour and beans. There was two cents change coming, and she used that to pay for a bag of jelly beans for Paul and Ruth. Her father would disapprove, she knew, but she just wouldn't say anything about it and neither would the kids.

She guessed she spoiled them some, but she was the only mother they'd known. Paul had been two when his mother died. She died giving birth to his sister, Ruth. Their mother was Elijah's second wife. She had sung in the choir when Elijah came to Endless to start his church here. That was two years after his first wife, Laura's mother, had died from typhoid fever when Laura was eight. Now Laura was seventeen, Paul was seven, and Ruth was five.

The next time Laura saw Link was at Sunday's church service. She was playing "Rock of Ages" at the pump organ. On the second chorus, she glanced out at the congregation and there he was on a bench near the back of the church. She stumbled over several notes. Elijah, standing at the pulpit preparing to start his sermon, gave her a reprimanding frown. Of course, he hadn't known the reason she'd made the mistake. He just thought she was being careless. If he'd suspected the true reason for her missing the notes, she would have been in real trouble.

After the service, when Laura was helping Elijah count the donations, they found a five-dollar gold piece in the collection plate. Elijah was stunned. He held the coin up, staring at it with awe. He gasped, "Praise the Lord!"

Who in the congregation could afford that kind of money? The community, depending on cattle ranches and cotton crops, had been hard hit with the drought that was now dragging into its third year. Elijah prayed for rain at every service, but so far the Lord hadn't heard him. Folks here were going through real hard times.

Laura suspected it was the curly-haired stranger who had spoken to her at the general store who put the gold piece in the collection plate. He looked the type who would carelessly toss money around. But she kept the thought to herself.

She took Paul and Ruth to the buckboard. Members of the church were congregated out in front of the church, visiting. Right out of the group came the stranger, strolling toward her with a lazy smile on his face. He leaned against the wagon, looking straight into her eyes. "You're a talented young lady in addition to being so pretty," he said. "That was real fine music you played on that organ."

The look from his eyes took Laura's breath away. He had some kind of power over her that made her knees weak. It was both exciting and frightening.

"My name's Link Houston," he said. "What's yours?"

"Laura," she stammered. "Laura Sontag."

"Laura," he repeated. "That sure is a pretty name. Pretty name for a pretty lady. Laura, would it be agreeable with you if I came calling some time?"

"I . . . I can't," she mumbled, pulling her gaze from his beautiful brown eyes. Her face was flushed. She cast her own eyes downward. "My father wouldn't permit it."

"Is there anywhere I could get to see you and talk to you some more?"

She swallowed hard. Without seeming to have any control of her voice, she blurted out, "The church is having a potluck dinner this evening here in the yard."

He smiled and winked. "Well, I might just come to that." Then he tipped his hat and went over to where his horse was tied. He swung into the saddle and waved to her and rode off.

Laura was so mesmerized that she stood on the spot, hardly aware of her surroundings until her father came up to her. "What were you doing talking to that man?" he demanded.

"We . . . we weren't exactly talking," she stammered. "He just came up to give me a compliment on how I played the organ."

Elijah had that dark look that told Laura he was displeased. "Laura, honey, that fellow is Link Houston. He's the no-good son of Ben Houston. He's a card-playing, harddrinking young man. Ben's had a lot of trouble with that boy. Maybe the boy can't help it. He grew up without a mother. I thought he'd left Endless for good, but now he's come back. Something about getting himself cut up in a knife fight over a card game, I heard. Anyway, it's best you don't have any truck with the likes of him."

"Yes, Papa," she said. She was disappointed that Link would be such a bad person. His eyes were so nice and warm, his smile so friendly. And she was sure he was the one who had put the five-dollar gold piece in the collection plate. Maybe her father was wrong about Link. She hoped so. Late that afternoon, before they left for the supper, she brushed her hair until it shone, then wound it up in a knot at the back of her neck. For once, she wished she had something better than the dress she'd made out of feed sacks. She thought wistfully about the bolt of material she'd seen at the store.

When the church members gathered around the picnic tables in the yard under the big old mesquite tree for the potluck supper, Laura was busy helping serve the meal. She kept glancing around, wondering if Link was going to come. She was secretly disappointed when she didn't see him. Then, her eyes darted toward the road. There he was, looking tall and splendid on his horse. He swung down and tied the horse. From his saddlebag he took a parcel. He brought it right up to her. "You said this was a potluck supper," he said with a smile. "I brought some barbecued beef."

"Thank you," she said, feeling self-conscious and tongue-tied. When she took the serving of beef from him, their hands touched. It sent a shiver all through her.

She stayed too busy with serving the meal to speak to him again. But afterward all the men went over to the site of the new church to do some carpenter work on the structure. The women went along to serve tea and punch when the men got thirsty. Link pitched in to saw boards and hammer nails. Once he came over to where she stood near the bucket of punch. She handed him a tin dipper full of the liquid. Fortunately, her father was on the other side of the building where he couldn't see them.

"Laura, I just have to visit you," he said. "I haven't

been able to get you out of my head since I first laid eyes on you at the general store. Is there any way?''

She drew a deep breath. She couldn't believe she would have such a wicked thought, but she could not stay away from Link Houston any more than she could stop breathing. ''Tonight,'' she blurted out, her voice low, her eyes darting around nervously. ''The gate at our place. By nine o'clock my father and the kids should be asleep. You know where we live, out the Mill Road?''

After the words were out, she was horrified. Had she actually said such a sinful thing? But another part of her was making her heart beat faster at the thought of talking to Link, getting to know him better.

He grinned broadly. ''I'll surely find it.'' He gave her hand a squeeze as he passed the dipper back to her. The squeeze sent a tingle shooting up her arm and all over her body.

As he walked away, Laura saw one of the women looking at her curiously. *Please don't let her tell Papa,* she prayed.

The next hours were the longest Laura had ever lived through. Back home after the church supper, they sat in the kitchen. Elijah read his Bible. Paul played with some wooden soldiers Elijah had carved for him. Ruth played with her rag doll. Laura mended clothes. She was so nervous, she repeatedly stuck her finger. From time to time, Elijah would clear his throat, lean back, and take his watch from his vest pocket. Laura wanted desperately to ask the time, but she was afraid to say anything that might make her father suspicious.

Once, their Border collie, Ranger, set up a dreadful barking out near the fence. Laura's blood ran cold. What if Link was out there now? What if her father went out to see what had got Ranger so all-fired stirred up? But then, to Laura's relief, the dog quieted down.

At long last, her father snapped his watch cover closed, announced that it was nine o'clock, and arose from his chair. They knelt for evening prayers. He kissed them all good night and went to his room. Laura took the children to the outhouse, carrying a lantern to make sure there were no rats there. Then she put them to bed. There were three rooms in the house. Elijah slept in one of the bedrooms. The children shared the other. The third room served as the kitchen and living area.

Laura got in her bed and pretended to go to sleep. Her body was rigid as she strained her ears for the steady breathing that would tell her Paul and Ruth were asleep. She couldn't believe what she was planning to do. She was miserable with guilt, yet unable to stop herself. The force that made her want to be with Link Houston overpowered all restraint.

Finally convinced the children were asleep, she got up and slipped into her dress and a pair of moccasins. As she started for the door, a floorboard creaked. Paul mumbled sleepily, "Where're you goin', Laura?"

"To the outhouse," she whispered. "Go back to sleep, Paul."

She stood frozen until he resumed his steady breathing.

In the kitchen, she listened at her father's door. His snoring assured her that he was sound asleep. Fortunately, he was a sound sleeper.

Outside, the yard was bathed in silver light from a full moon in a cloudless sky. Stars glittered like a billion diamonds. Only a Texas sky could have a canopy of so many hot, bright stars seemingly close enough to reach up and touch. All around the yard, fireflies blinked their own small starlight. "Lightning bugs," they were called.

There was the problem of Ranger. He came trotting out from near the barn where he slept and sniffed around her legs. "Ranger, go back," she ordered in a stern whisper. But he insisted on tagging along beside her. "You better be quiet, now." she warned. As if she wasn't nervous enough, she had the blamed dog to worry about!

Her other worry was the chickens. They were in their coops now, quiet enough, but if something spooked them and they raised a racket, her father was sure to wake up and come out to see if a possum or coyote had got in the chicken yard.

Laura hurried to the gate. Her heart was pounding wildly, her hands icy cold. It must be well after nine o'clock now. What if Link had grown tired of waiting and left? What if he'd never come at all? Maybe he was just having his fun, teasing a young girl who didn't know any better. He looked like the kind who liked to tease and have fun. He didn't look like one who'd take life very seriously.

She stood at the gatepost, straining her eyes, seeing nothing, feeling both relief and terrible disappointment.

Then she heard a soft whistle. He appeared as if by magic from a grove of mesquite trees off the road apiece and came up to the gate. She heard his horse snicker off in the grove of trees where he'd tied him.

"Hello, Laura," he said.

Seeing him again, she felt her heart gave a lurch.

To her surprise, Ranger went up to the gate, wagging his tail, giving a soft whimpering greeting. Link reached through the gate and rubbed the dog's head. "We made friends earlier tonight," he said. "I gave him some candy."

"It was you he was barking at," she said with surprise. "That was over an hour ago."

"I've been here at least that long," he said. "Reckon I'd have stayed the rest of the night, waiting, hoping you'd come."

"I don't have no business being here," she whispered. "I'm disobeying my father. 'Honor thy father and thy mother,' the Bible says. That makes me a sinner."

"Don't fret yourself that way," Link said. "It ain't no sin for a woman and man to have strong feelings for each other and have a wanting to be together. That's also in the Bible, ain't it?"

"I reckon," she said doubtfully.

He put his hands on the top rail of the gate and eased over it. His boots struck the ground with a soft "thud."

He came closer to her. "You're shivering, Laura," he murmured.

"I . . . I reckon I'm cold."

"But it's a warm night."

The next thing she knew, he had put his arms around her, drawing her close. She felt the warmth of his body close against hers. It stirred up pleasurable, yearning sensations inside her that she had never before experienced. The sensations were overpowering.

"Laura, you're the prettiest, most wonderful girl I ever met," he said, his voice sounding hoarse. "You need to forgive me if I don't say things exactly right. I'm not used to being with a girl like you who reads the Bible and comes from a respectable home."

"My father says you're not respectable," she said, feeling nervous, sad, and happy all at the same time. "He says you play cards and drink hard liquor."

"I reckon he's right about the cards," Link admitted. "I take a drink now and then, but I'm not what you'd call a drinking man. It's true about the cards, though. I won't lie to you."

"But, but . . . cards. They were put here by the devil. They're sinful."

"Sure are the way they been runnin' for me lately," he admitted ruefully. "Laura, everything you say about me is true. But I could change for someone like you. Can you believe that?"

"I . . . I'd like to."

"Then believe it. There isn't much I wouldn't do for you, girl."

That was the first of many stolen meetings out at the

gatepost. One night, it began sprinkling. They ran to the barn to stay dry. Link persuaded Laura to lie down beside him on a pile of soft hay and snuggle up warm and close in his arms.

Laura didn't think she ever wanted to leave Link's strong arms. They talked far into the night, making wonderful plans. Somehow, Link promised, he was either going to get the money to pay off the loan on his father's land or convince the banker to extend the note. When it was paid off, Link was sure his father would let him build a house on the land and help with the ranching. Then he and Laura could get married.

That night, Link kissed her for the first time. Her father would say it was a sin to be lying in a man's arms this way and kissing, but it didn't seem so. It was sweet and right. She was so filled with joy her throat ached and her cheeks were damp with tears of happiness.

The dreams turned to tragedy. The next week Laura heard the terrible news. Link had been arrested for the murder of the banker, Albert Milam.

The worst part was that she couldn't ask what was happening to Link. She desperately clutched at every scrap of gossip she heard at the general store or at church. She did get the courage to ask her father if she could take some homemade food to the prisoner, convincing Elijah it would be an act of Christian charity. Her father would not permit her to visit the jail, but he agreed to take a basket of food that she prepared to the prisoner. She hid a note in the pie she baked, telling Link that she knew he was innocent, and that she was praying for him night and day.

Laura couldn't eat. Her nights were filled with frightening dreams. She turned thin as a rail. Her face was tired and drawn. Her haunted eyes were underlined with dark circles.

At Sunday service, while seated at the organ, she fainted. They carried her outside into the fresh air. She was aware of the women ministering to her, shaking their heads. She knew the congregation had decided that she had contracted a fatal lung disease. Her father was grim with worry. He asked the congregation to pray for her healing.

She couldn't tell anyone the real reason. Her father was a good, kind man. His life was devoted to helping others. When one of his flock was in need, he'd give anything he had, chickens, eggs, pigs, even if it meant his own family barely having food for their own table. But he could also be stern with his children if he thought it best for them, and that was why, from the beginning, he had strictly forbidden Laura to have anything to do with Link Houston.

The town was convinced that Link Houston would be hanged. He couldn't afford a good lawyer to defend him. The defense lawyer the court appointed, Victor Crenshaw, was incompetent and half senile.

It had been expected that the jury would come right back with a verdict that would get Link hung. Instead, they wrangled for two days and finally agreed on a lesser manslaughter charge that brought a prison sentence instead of a hangman's noose. Many folks were outraged. The town had been cheated out of a hanging. There was some talk of a lynching. The sheriff nervously hired extra deputies to guard Link's jail cell.

Today, much to the sheriff's relief, the three o'clock stage rolled out of town, taking Link Houston to Huntsville.

Now, as Laura rode the wagon through the storm on her way home, she could no longer ignore the tornado bearing down on the town. She saw the black mass in the sky, saw the giant tail licking the ground, heard the roar of a dozen steam locomotives. The wagon rattled over the cattle guard into the yard. Laura jumped off the seat and hurried into the house. The children were alone. Elijah was at the site of the new church, trying to get the last boards on the roof.

Paul and Ruth came running to Laura. They were terrified. Paul's face was white. Ruth was sobbing. The roaring had grown so loud, they couldn't hear her speak. She knew they had to act fast. Fortunately, the old house had a cellar. She opened the trapdoor, pulled the children down the steps, and closed the door above them.

They huddled together in the darkness. Above them, they heard the enormous force like a freight train smash into the house. They heard the splintering crash of boards, felt the suction that took the breath out of their lungs. Ruth screamed. Paul held onto Laura's neck with all his strength. Laura could only kneel and pray as she waited for them to die.

Chapter Three

The sky had turned threatening early on the morning the tornado struck. When Elijah Sontag went out to milk the cow, he saw the sunrise sending shafts between banks of heavy clouds. As the morning wore on, the clouds grew darker and the wind picked up. Scattered showers sprinkled raindrops on the dry dust of the land. Gathering storm clouds promised a deluge before the day ended.

"Praise the Lord," Elijah cried. He fell on his knees in the yard and thanked God for this sign that the terrible drought was ending.

He quickly hitched up the buckboard. One section of the new church roof was not completed. He needed to cover the opening before the heavy rain came. He loaded his tools in the wagon and called for Laura to drive him into town.

35

He wanted her to buy some candles, matches, kerosene oil for the lamps and a bag of flour from the store and get back before the road became too muddy. He would stay at the church until the rainstorm ended.

Laura was thankful for reasons other than the rain. Today, they were taking Link away to Huntsville. This would be her last chance to see him. She had been unable to think of a plausible reason for going into town. Now circumstances had arranged it for her.

They drove the short distance into Endless, arriving at noon. At the site of the new church, Elijah unloaded his tools. Laura left him there and drove the wagon to the store on Main Street. On the way, she passed the sheriff's office and jail. She stared at the building, hoping desperately to catch a glimpse of Link, but she was disappointed. A small crowd had already gathered on the boardwalk in front of the store. The stagecoach would stop here. The sheriff and his deputies would bring Link out of the jail down the street and escort him to the waiting stage, standing guard until the stage was on its way out of town.

Laura made her few purchases, but she did not start home immediately, as her father had instructed. Instead, she hung around the store, trying to look as inconspicuous as possible as she waited to catch a farewell glimpse of Link. It was the saddest day of her life.

At the site of the new church building, Elijah propped a ladder against the building. By then, the rain was coming down in steady sheets. He wore a ragged old slicker which afforded very little protection. He didn't care about getting soaked. His only concern was to secure the section of the roof to protect the interior of the church. They had tacked a tarp over the opening for temporary protection, but the way the wind was picking up, it would soon be ripped off. The opening had to be securely covered with planks.

This new church building was the greatest achievement of Elijah Sontag's ministry. It was the answer to a thousand prayers. Ever since he'd come to Endless and started his church here, services had been held in a ramshackle, abandoned barn on the edge of town. It was a poor place to serve as a church. The floor was hard-packed dirt. The roof leaked badly. No matter how much wood the elders piled into the potbellied stove, the place was cold in the winter.

With his gaunt, craggy features, lanky six-foot-four frame, and intense, piercing black eyes, Elijah Sontag bore a remarkable resemblance to Abraham Lincoln. He always wore a black suit, white shirt, and black shoestring tie. On a cold winter day, when he stood on the platform preaching, his words formed clouds of vapor in the frigid air. He truly looked like a fire-breathing prophet out of the Old Testament.

But that was changing at last. It had taken many years of saving pennies and nickels from the collection plate, but the church finally had the funds to buy a plot of land and enough lumber. With the elders helping, Elijah was building a real church. It was almost finished. When he got these boards on the roof, it would be protected from the elements. One of his parishioners, a cabinetmaker by trade, had, in his spare time, built a beautiful altar. There were real glass windows and a hardwood floor. It was truly a church that would make Endless proud.

Life had not been easy for Elijah Sontag. He had grown up the son of a poor circuit-riding preacher. He had known poverty all of his life. When he was twenty-one, he felt the call to preach the word as his father had done. Whatever his hardships, he never wavered from his call. He was convinced he was put on earth to be a servant to the sick and the needy and to preach the word of God.

The Lord had blessed him with a faithful wife, Clementine. She had given him a lovely daughter, Laura. When Laura was eight, the Lord had taken Clementine during the typhoid epidemic.

It was a terrible loss. Elijah was wracked with grief, but he accepted it as God's will. Because of the sad memories in the town where his wife died, he had moved to Endless. At that time, there was not a single church in the town. Weddings and funerals were conducted by a circuit-riding preacher like his father had been.

Endless was a rough frontier town, but they had brought in a strong sheriff, Matt Blake, who established some law and order. An element of law-abiding folks wanted a church and welcomed a preacher who would settle there.

Elijah took a second wife, Eloise Jones, a young widow who was blessed with a beautiful singing voice. She led the choir in Elijah's newly established church. They were married a year when she gave him a son, Paul. Two years later, she was pregnant again. Once more, tragedy struck. She died giving birth to their daughter, Ruth.

Elijah held a strong belief in the wages of sin. If one suffered sickness or a loss or any kind of misfortune, Elijah believed it was God's punishment for a sin of some kind in one's life.

He became convinced that both wives had been taken from him because of his sins. Somehow, he had not been faithful enough, had not prayed hard enough, had not rid his mind of sinful and lustful thoughts. He had poured himself with even greater intensity into his ministry, trying his utmost to be a good father to his children while at the same time ministering to the needs of his congregation. His efforts must have pleased God, he thought, for he had been rewarded with this fine church building.

It was with a great feeling of relief that he drove the last nail into the roof. Now the church would be snug and dry while the rainstorm raged. With the drought broken, ranchers would prosper and the church would grow. He was soaked to the skin but wonderfully happy.

And then he heard the roaring sound. He turned. His eyes grew wide and his face turned white as he saw the huge, black, funnel-shaped cloud with its tail licking the earth, headed straight for Endless. He knew at once it was a tornado.

He scrambled down from the roof. He ran to a ditch a few hundred yards away and flung himself into it. The roaring grew louder. The breath was sucked from his lungs. Debris was flying everywhere. He stared in horror at the church building. It was ripped to shreds, turned into matchsticks, flung in all directions.

"No!" Elijah screamed. He left the safety of the ditch, running toward the splintering building. The awful wind sent him sprawling in the mud. He struggled to his knees, attempting to pray. A flying board smashed the back of his head, knocking him down.

He fell into a pit of blackness darker than the evil wind that had destroyed his church.

Chapter Four

The morning of the storm, attorney Victor Crenshaw was seated at the table in the Sunset Saloon in Endless. He was on his third glass of bourbon, sipping the liquor as he stared somberly at the gusts of wind-driven rain splattering against the saloon window. In spite of the liquor he had consumed that morning, he made a determined effort to sit upright in a dignified manner befitting a man of the legal profession. As always, he was dressed in the style he deemed suited to a gentleman of the bar. Although there were food stains on the shirt and the coat sleeves were frayed, his attire was a black frock coat and white linen shirt.

Across the street, his sign, VICTOR CRENSHAW, ATTORNEY AT LAW, hung outside the tiny, cluttered office above the general store, was banging back and forth violently in

41

the wind. Victor gazed at it moodily. He raised his glass in a mock salute. His lips formed the words. "Victor Crenshaw, Attorney at Law." He laughed bitterly, downed the liquor and started on his fourth glass.

It was a sad day. It was the day they were taking young Link Houston to the Huntsville state prison where he'd serve hard time.

All of his adult life, Victor Crenshaw had been haunted with the demoralizing knowledge that he was a fraud and a failure. Somehow he'd garnered enough legal knowledge to write up wills and deeds and handle minor civil suits, but he was no real lawyer. Never had he faced the awesome task of defending a man's life until he was appointed by the court to represent young Link Houston in the murder trial. He had begged the judge not to put the burden on him, but the court wouldn't be budged. There was no other lawyer in Endless. If Link wanted a better defense lawyer, he'd have to bring one in from San Antonio. Neither Link nor his father could scrape together that kind of money. So they were saddled with Victor Crenshaw, who knew almost nothing about criminal law.

Victor had got out his dusty old law books and tried his best to study them, but the words wouldn't stay in his mind. The complicated legal concepts he tried to grasp were lost in a fog. He was seventy-five and it was getting hard to remember things. But age wasn't the real problem. The truth was that he'd never been much of a lawyer. He knew he was no match for the sharp young prosecutor from San

Antonio that Sid Milam had hired to convict the man who had murdered his brother.

Victor believed Link when the boy swore he was innocent. That frustrated him the most. An innocent young man was being railroaded and Victor Crenshaw was too incompetent to save his client. If he'd been a real lawyer, he could have convinced the jury how flimsy the state's case was, based on witnesses who'd seen Link quarrel with Milam earlier in the day and the testimony of a man known to be the town drunk. He did know enough to tell the jury the state's case was all circumstantial evidence, but they didn't seem to pay much attention to him.

Tears ran down Victor's cheeks when he begged the jury not to hang this innocent boy. Rather than moving the jury, it just embarrassed them. They saw a doddering old fool blubbering because he didn't know the right legal terms.

Victor had stumbled through the closing argument, forgetting at times what he was trying to say. By contrast, the slick prosecutor from San Antonio held the jury mesmerized. He asked for the death penalty, and it looked to Victor that most of the men on the jury agreed.

The judge told the jury they had three choices: they could find Link innocent; they could find him guilty of murder with malice aforethought; or they could find him guilty of a lesser degree of manslaughter.

When the jury went out, Victor sat slumped in his seat. He couldn't look at his client. He knew what the verdict was going to be. In his mind, Victor could hear the hammers and saws building the gallows in back of the jail.

Like everyone else in the courtroom, Victor expected the jury to return with a death sentence verdict within the hour. They were out for two days. That surprised and confused Victor. It baffled the town. What was holding up the jury? Everyone was sure there was going to be a hanging.

Finally, the jury came in. They looked tired and mad. When they read their verdict of a lesser manslaughter charge, the courtroom exploded with enraged shouts. The judge looked furious. The young prosecutor was red-faced with anger. Victor was simply stunned.

Ben Houston thanked Victor for saving his son's life. Victor had stared at him blankly. As confused as he was, he knew he hadn't saved anything. Why had the jury spared Link from the gallows? It was a question that baffled Victor Crenshaw as much as anyone. Something very strange had happened in that jury.

A shocking thought nagged the back of Victor's mind. Had somebody gotten to the jury? Was it possible some of the jurors had been bribed? He thought there were men on the jury who might accept a bribe. But who would pay them to save Link from getting his neck stretched?

It was a mystery that troubled Victor. He kept quiet about it, though. If the judge threw out the verdict and ordered a new trial, Link would surely hang. Anyway, if one or more men on the jury had taken a bribe, they sure weren't going to admit it. Taking that kind of bribe was a serious offense.

Was the real killer involved in tampering with the jury? It was an intriguing thought. Victor wished he could somehow pursue the matter, but he didn't know how. Besides, he was afraid. Someone beside Link Houston had killed the banker. He could easily kill again. If Victor went nosing around, he could very well get a bullet through his brain. So, besides being a fraud as a lawyer, Victor Crenshaw was also a coward. All he could do was sit here and listen to the storm outside while he tried to numb his sense of failure with liquor.

Finally, it got to be three in the afternoon. Victor arose with as much dignity as he could muster as he walked unsteadily outside and joined the men on the board sidewalk, watching them put the prisoner in the stagecoach. Link's father was there, telling the young man goodbye. Victor thought he should say something to them, tell them how sorry he was that he had failed them. But he just stood there, watching.

Victor noticed a young woman back away from the curious crowd, near the doorway of the general store. The lawyer recognized her as the daughter of the preacher, Elijah Sontag. He'd heard some gossip around town that she and Link had been sweethearts. Victor saw a look of grief on her pretty young face. She was crying quietly. Another thing to add to Victor's burden.

The stage pulled away, the team sloshing down the muddy street. The men went back inside the saloon to get out of the rain. Victor ordered another bottle of liquor. A few more drinks, he knew, would turn off the hurting part of his mind. He'd had a lot of practice doing that.

It was about thirty minutes later when a man rushed into

the saloon yelling something about a tornado coming.
There was a stampede. Men knocked chairs and tables over
in their haste to get outside. Victor took his time.

Outside, people were pointing to the sky. Men were running in all directions. Victor heard shouts and screams. He
looked up at the thing. It was a terrifying sight, the blackest
cloud he had ever seen, a kind of whirling vortex making
a deafening sound. It seemed to fill the entire sky as it came
closer.

Victor watched it for a moment, then went back inside
the saloon. He had the place to himself now. He poured
himself a fresh drink. It had grown as dark as night. The
entire room was vibrating.

He could no longer see the sign across the street, VICTOR
CRENSHAW, ATTORNEY AT LAW. It had blown down.

Victor's mind turned backward, remembering many
things, times when he was a child on the farm in Virginia,
his father and mother, the children he played with at school,
the women he had known, his many business failures, his
wife who had died ten years ago.

He raised his glass. He toasted the memories, the good
times and the bad times. He toasted a life that had been a
failure.

He thought about Link Houston. He wished he knew
what had happened to the jury. He wished he knew who
had really killed Albert Milam.

The tornado struck. In seconds, the Sunset Saloon was
turned into a pile of kindling wood.

Chapter Five

Ben Houston rode out of Endless immediately after telling Link goodbye. He rode slumped in the saddle, unmindful of the rain pelting him. The storm raging inside him made him oblivious of the dangerous weather outside.

He'd always expected that Link was headed for a no-good end. The boy had a wild, reckless streak and a talent for getting into trouble that Ben couldn't tame. As Link grew into a husky teenager, he'd become harder and harder to manage. Finally, Link left home to become a drifter and gambler. That changed a couple of months ago, when he had come home with a knife wound in his gut. Link got himself a girlfriend, the respectable daughter of the preacher, no less. Ben was beginning to think that maybe the close brush with death had made Link grow up at last.

Was it possible that the worthless kid might straighten himself out and have a future?

Then Link took it on himself to get involved in the trouble Ben was having with the bank. In his usual reckless, hotheaded manner, Link had a violent confrontation with the banker. There had been angry words, threats. That night, Albert Milam was murdered and now Link was on his way to prison.

Ben wasn't entirely convinced that his son was innocent. Link seemed sincere when he swore he'd had nothing to do with the murder. But it was hard for Ben to forget the many times in the past that Link had lied to him and disappointed him. It would not have been out of character for Link to go back to face Albert Milam that night, get in another name-calling ruckus and, in a reckless moment, pull his gun. It was also typical of Link to try and run away when he heard he was going to be charged with the murder.

Still, Ben wanted to give the kid the benefit of the doubt. He couldn't forget that Link's trouble had come about because of Ben's problem with the bank mortgage.

Suddenly realizing that he was getting wet, Ben held his reins in his teeth for a moment while he drew his slicker tighter with his one hand. Hell of a rainstorm. Reminded him of all the times he'd been wet and cold and hungry during the war between the states.

More than twenty years had passed since Appomatox, but for Ben Houston the war had never ended. He'd left more than his right arm at Gettysburg. He'd left part of who he was back there. There were losses that wouldn't heal. The loss of so many friends. The loss of pride. It was hell to lose a war. It made all the sacrifices, deaths, and destruction pointless.

Every night he had dreams about Pickett's futile charge up Cemetery Ridge at Gettysburg that had cost the Confederacy the war.

Up to that point, Robert E. Lee had been the most brilliant military strategist either side had produced. Despite being outnumbered and outgunned by Union forces, Lee had led his ragged army of Rebs to one victory after another.

By July of 1863, both the North and South were exhausted by the war. There were protest riots in northern cities. The South was being strangled by the Yankee blockade of southern ports. The Confederacy was desperately short of food and supplies.

The South's only hope was that England and France might come in on the side of the Confederacy.

There was good reason for Lee to invade Pennsylvania. A major Southern victory on Northern soil might turn public sentiment in the North so strongly against continuing the war that open rebellion could force Washington to agree to peace terms.

Maybe that was Lee's fateful decision, to gamble everything on Pickett's charge across that vast, open field, up Cemetery Ridge. If successful, the charge could have ended the war between the states. But it was doomed from the start.

Everything had gone wrong. Jeb Stuart, Lee's dashing

cavalry leader, had been off on a foraging expedition instead of at Gettysburg, where Lee needed him. With his usual daring skill, Stuart could have reconnoitered, probed the Union's strength and weak points. But he got to Gettysburg too late to be of any help.

Lee had believed his artillery could demolish the Union forces on Cemetery Ridge. One hundred and seventy Confederate guns were lined up along the edge of the woods facing the ridge and, at 1:00 P.M. began the fiercest bombardment in the nation's history. But the smoke was so dense the gunners couldn't accurately gauge where the shells were landing. Much of the barrage went past the Union troops lined up along the ridge. The Confederate gunners could have used one of those newfangled balloon observers to direct their fire.

Then, in the stifling ninety-degree heat of that July afternoon, General Pickett, obeying Lee's orders, began the charge.

Ben clearly remembered that long march across the vast open field, remembered the weight of his Enfield rifle, saw the sunlight glinting off the bayonet, heard the shout of a lieutenant, "Home, boys, Home! Remember, home is over beyond those hills!"

There were so many marching beside him, 12,000 men in the ragtag butternut gray Confederate uniforms, keeping their ranks in order—a sight no man who saw it could ever forget.

And then came the sheets of withering artillery and rifle fire from the ridge. Around Ben, his friends fell by the hundreds like a field of grain swept by a giant scythe. In less than an hour, 7,500 Confederate soldiers fell. A mini ball hit Ben like a sledgehammer, knocking him flat.

At first he'd felt no pain, just numbness all over. He was conscious. He looked up at the clear sky above. Around him, the sounds of the battle, the whistling of mini balls, the thunder of Union artillery, the screams of the wounded, the rattle of musket fire, were deafening. Then his pain began and he screamed along with the others on the blood-soaked ground around him.

Pickett's charge failed. Lee took the remnants of his army back across the Potomac to Virginia. The war dragged on another year, but the Confederacy was beaten.

Ben lay on the field half out of his mind with pain for most of the afternoon. Eventually, he was carried to a field hospital behind the enemy lines where a Union surgeon amputated his arm. The heavy mini balls shattered bones into so many fragments, there was no choice but amputation. The severed arms and legs stacked around the operating table under the tree were knee-high that day.

Many soldiers died from shock, overdose of chloroform or blood poisoning after an amputation. But Ben survived the operation and the Union prison and eventually came home to his ranch at Endless.

He'd come back a broken man to try to learn all over how to make a living as a rancher with only one arm. He guessed he could understand why his wife, Margaret, left him for another man. He must have been hell to live with in those days. What he couldn't forgive her for was her leaving Link for him to raise. If the boy'd had a mother, he might have turned out to be a better man.

He was so filled with the bitter memories now as he rode home that he'd hadn't paid much attention to the storm. He hadn't looked around to see the black, funnel-shaped cloud bearing down on him. He had almost reached the ranch when the tornado struck. It was the earsplitting sound that aroused him. He spilled out of the saddle and hit the ground. His horse whinnied in terror and bolted.

Ben was on his belly, crawling across an open field. The cyclone made all the racket of an artillery barrage. Scraps of lumber and tin whistled through the air like cannon shells and mini balls. The awful wind pounded Ben and sucked the breath out of him. In the nightmare he thought he heard commanding officers yelling orders. He saw Billy Joe Simmons clutch at his throat and fall beside him, vomiting blood. He saw his sergeant on the ground, his head blown apart, brains splattered in the grass.

Ben screamed the Rebel yell. He drew his six-gun, firing as he slithered along the ground toward a small rise two hundred yards away. "Charge, boys!" he cried. "Over that ridge is home!"

Chapter Six

Link stumbled through wounded fields. Trees, stripped of bark and leaves, were skeletons. Their bony arms were stretched in a plea for mercy to a sky that had gone mad. Mud sucked at Link's boots. Rain still fell in blinding sheets. A hailstorm followed on the heels of the tornado. Link was knocked down by stones as large as a man's fist. Half stunned, he crawled along like an animal, beaten and bruised by the stoning.

Finally, the hailstorm passed, tagging along behind the tornado cloud.

He knew the tornado must have reached Endless by now. In the distance, he could see lumber flying through the air. He thought of Laura's slender body being hurled like a rag

53

doll. His eyes burned. Tears ran down his muddy, blood-streaked cheeks.

As the hailstorm eased, he saw a pile of lumber not far away. By now his leg was in such pain, he didn't try to use the crutch. He crawled to the wreckage, struggling through the mud and debris, dragging his tree-limb crutch behind him. When he got there, he saw that it was all that was left of what had been a small ranch house.

Someone was looking up at him between the boards. He clawed the boards away. The person looking up at him was a woman. She was dead.

He strained to lift and drag other boards aside. He found two more bodies, a man and a small child. After that, he didn't look any more. No one was alive there.

There was another pile of wreckage in the yard, a hundred yards or so away. It was the remains of the barn. At a further distance, near a fringe of trees on the outer rim of the twister's path was a corral. It had survived. So had several horses penned there.

Link crawled to the wreckage of the barn. He found a bridle. Then, gritting his teeth, he used the makeshift crutch to limp his way painfully to the corral. By then his left boot had become as tight as a vise. That meant the bottom half of his left leg was swelling like a puffed-up toad.

With great effort, Link managed to get a bridle on one of the horses. He mounted it bareback. He guided the horse to the corral gate, leaned down, and opened the gate. As he rode out, he didn't bother to close the gate. If the other horses were left penned in the corral, they'd starve. There was no one left here to take care of them.

He supposed he was horse-stealing, but the people in the demolished house had no further use for horses. By now he knew that, with his injured leg getting worse at every step, he'd never make it back to Endless on foot.

On the horse, he made good time. The tornado had cut a path in a straight line to Endless. When he got closer, Link skirted what was the remains of the town. His destination was the Mill Road where the Sontag family lived.

All fences were gone. The road was covered with debris and fallen mesquite trees.

Then he came to where Laura's home had stood. The gate where they had their stolen meetings was gone. The house was a pile of boards and rubble.

With an awful feeling in the pit of his stomach, Link urged his horse closer, dismounted, and tied the reins over a broken tree branch. He limped to the ruins of the house.

When he scrambled over the boards, he heard faint cries coming from somewhere under the pile of rubble. The pain in his throbbing leg was forgotten as he frantically began ripping boards away.

Chapter Seven

The tornado missed the ranch of Sid Milam, which was several miles from town. Milam stood on the porch of the sprawling stone home and watched the storm. It had a tail like a giant scorpion that reached down to sting the main street of Endless. He knew the venom in that tail was killing the town.

He was badly shaken. On a corner of Main Street was his bank, one of the few brick buildings in town. He'd had it built just two years ago. Most of the structures along Main Street were adobe or flimsy frame buildings with false fronts. A storm like that would turn them into matchsticks. Would his brick bank building survive? He doubted it.

Sid Milam thought of the money in the bank. Most of it

was in the vault. Had the bank teller, Jake Simms, had sense enough to put the money from the cash drawer into the vault and slam shut the heavy door?

Sid Milam was a worried man. He worried about the bank building. He worried about whether the vault door had been closed.

What he was mostly worried about was looters. The word sent a chill through his veins.

Gusts of wind and rain were making the front porch uncomfortable. He went inside the house and poured himself a drink of expensive bourbon. His wife, Angelita, was standing near a window, watching the storm.

Sid Milam looked at her with brooding eyes as he swallowed his drink. Although now in her early thirties, she was still a beautiful woman. The rich, haughty ancestry of her pure Spanish heritage was visible in her clear complexion, her high, smooth forehead, large, luminous dark eyes, sensuous lips and the long, clean lines of her throat.

Angelita Torres—daughter of Cruz Torres, who had been the richest rancher in this section of the state, his land grants going back to the days of the Spanish crown. Sid Milam considered marrying Cruz Torres's daughter as his greatest achievement and biggest stroke of luck. The marriage made Sid one of the richest men in Texas after old man Torres died. Angelita had been his only living child and heir. Technically, she owned the land, but in Texas in 1889, a woman had few rights. Angelita knew nothing about business. It was no trick to get her signature on papers that for all practical purposes put the land in Sid's name. She had a small fortune in jewelry tucked away here and there, but Sid didn't bother with that. It had been the land he was after.

All things considered, the Civil War had been the best thing that happened in Sid Milam's life. Had it not been for that conflict and the reconstruction of the South that followed, Sid would today probably be grubbing away as a law clerk in Boston for a measly salary.

He had been smart to seize the political opportunities following the devastation of the War. In those first years, Southerners were stripped of voting rights. A man of undisputed Union loyalty could come down and grab a lot of political power. There were many war widows left with mortgages on their land and nothing to pay them off with but worthless Confederate bonds and cash. Sid Milam saw the chance to make himself rich. He picked this isolated town of Endless as a good hunting ground. He could see himself owning the town and most of the land around it in no time at all. He bought up mortgages for ten cents on the dollar, then foreclosed. Some of the land that he acquired, he sold to Northern investors for hard gold coins. With that money, he started the town's only bank.

The richest prize in the entire area was Cruz Torres's vast ranch, but there was no way Sid could have acquired it short of marrying Cruz Torres's only daughter. There was no mortgage on the property, and Torres had been a Union sympathizer during the war. His son had gone North to fight for the Union and was killed at Fredericksburg, leaving Angelita the only heir.

Sid had courted her assiduously. Fortunately, Cruz Torres took a liking to him. The Spanish landowner, once a fierce young vaquero, had grown old with many of the infirmities that come with age. He knew his days were numbered. His great sorrow was the loss of his only son who would have one day owned the ranch. Now it would go to Angelita.

He would certainly have preferred that Angelita marry a man of Hispanic heritage. But the available *tejanos* were mostly cowboys, few with any sense to manage the big ranch.

Cruz was good at measuring men. True, Sid Milam was a gringo, a hard nut for Cruz to swallow. But Cruz respected Milam's shrewd business and political know-how. It was obvious that Sid Milam was rapidly becoming the most powerful man in Endless. He would be the big *patrón*, the man who told others how to vote, the man who picked the officials in the town, the mayor, the sheriff, the county judge. When a man wanted to run for state senator or representative, he would have to come to Sid Milam for support. Such a man as Sid Milam would give Angelita the position and respect Cruz wanted for her. He would know how to make the Torres ranch continue to prosper so it could one day pass on to Angelita's children.

Angelita had never loved Sid Milam, but she was an obedient daughter who followed the customs of her heritage and obeyed her father in such matters. She accepted Sid Milam's proposal of marriage. It was the most lavish wedding the town had ever seen and the fiesta that followed at the Cruz Torres ranch went on for days. Not long after,

Cruz Torres died believing he had done the right thing for his daughter.

Yes, Sid Milam often thought, marrying Angelita had been the crowning achievement of his career. But it was not without thorns. Angelita did not love him. She never showed the slightest passion in his embrace. She was like an ice statue who accepted his lovemaking as an onerous chore. That was a grueling wound to his ego, especially in view of the fact that he was obsessed with her beauty. He was insanely jealous of the thought that somewhere in the world there might be a man who could awaken the fire she denied him. The fact that she bore him no child did not make matters any easier for him.

But today there were other concerns on his mind. All the cash he had in the world was in his bank in Endless. If looters got to it, he would be a ruined man. It would take years for the town to rebuild. The property and businesses he owned in town would be gone. The land around Endless would be worthless. He had to protect the bank vault at all costs.

"I'm going into town," he told Angelita. "I have to guard the bank."

She didn't look at him. She just gave him a brief shrug.

He glared at her. There were times when, out of frustration, he had slapped her. She hadn't given him the satisfaction of crying. She'd just given him that cold, haughty stare. Right now was one of the times he felt like hitting her. But there were more pressing matters.

He put on a slicker and went outside. He ordered a ranch

hand to saddle his horse. He began his ride to guard the remains of his bank in Endless. He had a shotgun in his saddle holster.

Riding toward the remains of the town, Sid Milam was filled with apprehension. He had the premonition that the tornado was some kind of evil thing that, having wrecked the town, was going to bring disaster to everyone who lived here. And he had the awful fear that he was not immune from that evil.

Chapter Eight

Since most of the trees in this arid part of Texas were scraggly mesquite and huisache, Endless had started out as a tiny settlement of adobe buildings clustered around an ancient Spanish Mission like chicks around a mother hen. In the early days, the town had often been the target of Indian raids and Mexican bandits crossing the river. Later, as the town began to grow, lumber was brought in by oxcart and wagon train. Frame buildings sprang up along Main Street, between the old adobe huts: a meat market, barbershop, drugstore, real estate office, restaurant, dance hall, newspaper, livery stable, and blacksmith. Two years ago, the most imposing building on Main Street, Sid Milam's two-story First City Bank, was constructed from brick brought in from San Antonio, and floor tile brought from Mexico. Six months ago construction was begun on a three-story brick and stone county courthouse. It was half finished.

When the tornado hit Endless, young Doctor Claus von Blucher was five miles away, delivering a baby to the family of Manuel and Sarita Cortez, the seventh in their healthy brood of boys. It was not a difficult birth; nevertheless, Claus had been too busy to pay attention to the weather outside other than to be aware of a heavy downpour beating the tin roof of the modest Cortez home.

When the child had been safely delivered and placed in the arms of his perspiring but happy mother, the young doctor went out to the kitchen where the father was seated at a table with two of his cousins, drinking tequila.

With the limited amount of Spanish that Claus had been able to pick up since coming to Texas six months ago, he managed to convey to Manuel Cortez that he was the father of a healthy boy. That brought a whoop of joy from the men at the table. Manuel jumped up and gave the doctor a rib-crushing *abrazo*, at the same time knocking the breath out of him by pounding his back. There was a lot of excited talk, none of which Claus von Blucher understood, and some more tequila drinking. Then Manuel went in to meet his son. Dr. von Blucher put on his slicker, picked up his medical bag, and started for the door.

"*Muy malo*," one of the cousins told him with a serious look, shaking his head. He went to the door with von Blucher and pointed in the direction of Endless. "Very bad. I see. *Una* storm *grande*," he said in the Tex-Mex mixture of Spanish and English. "I see. I watch." He made a fist in the air, brought it down on his palm with a hard "smack!" Again he shook his head. "Endless. *Pobrecito. Yo creo que el pueblo está muerto.*"

Claus struggled to grasp his meaning. He recognized the words *pueblo* and *muerto*. They meant "town" and "dead." What was the man trying to tell him? Something about a storm.

He felt a sense of foreboding as he went out to the shed, hitched up his buggy and started his ride back to Endless.

"*Vaya con Dios*," the cousin told him sadly as the doctor rode out of the yard.

The Cortez family lived on the road to Laredo. It was topped with caliche which caused clouds of dust in dry weather but provided a solid roadbed during heavy rains.

The rain was a blessing, the doctor thought. Maybe it would be the end of the drought and some of the patients he had treated the past six months would be able to start paying the bills they owed him.

Claus came from a wealthy, aristocratic German family. After completing his medical studies at the finest universities Europe had to offer, he had fulfilled a lifelong ambition to come to America.

In New York, he had started his practice. There, he'd fallen in love with a beautiful young American woman, Cindy Markey. They were to be married in a month. Then she contracted yellow fever. Despite his impressive medical degrees, he could do nothing to save her. She died in his arms.

Heartbroken, he packed up his books and medical equipment and bought a train ticket for Texas. He planned to start a new life at one of the German settlements in Texas, possibly New Braunfels on the Comal River.

However, when he arrived in Austin, he was told about Endless, a small West Texas town near the Rio Grande that urgently needed a doctor. There wasn't another doctor within a hundred miles. The only medical treatment available there were midwives and the Mexican *curanderos*, who practiced folk remedies.

He got the notion that fate had shaped his life to bring him here to Endless where a doctor was so urgently needed. When he left New York City, he'd sought an existence as far as possible from the life he had known. He had certainly found it in this remote corner of Texas.

The quiet, cultured, well-educated young doctor had been welcomed by the community. The people were open and friendly. Their rough frontier manners were a world away from the sophisticated people he had known in Europe, but he liked their honesty and decency. He'd opened a drugstore. In the back was his examining room and surgical table. He had the latest medical equipment shipped here. Above the store was a room where he cooked his meals and slept.

He didn't sleep much. His services were urgently needed. At all hours of the day and night, he set cowboys' broken bones, lanced boils, operated on gunshot victims, treated snake bites, delivered babies. His practice took him all over the area in his buggy or on horseback.

Now, as he approached Endless, the rain was letting up. Some rays from the sun were beginning to send shafts through the storm-torn clouds.

He rounded the last bend in the road. Then he went numb with shock. He drew back on the reins. His eyes behind his wire-rimmed glasses were wide with shock. The town he had left this morning now looked like a village of card houses that had been knocked flat and scattered by a giant fist.

"*Ach, du lieber Gott,*" he gasped. For a moment, he was too horrified to move. Was this what Manuel Cortez's cousin was trying to tell him about a terrible storm that had killed Endless?

How could something like this happen? He'd heard the rain and wind gusts. But no ordinary storm could cause this kind of destruction. Then he remembered reading about the kind of windstorms called tornadoes or cyclones that struck some parts of the United States. Was that what had happened here?

Rousing himself from his daze, he slapped the reins on his horse's rump. The buggy rolled forward, but it was soon stopped by the wreckage. Main Street was impassible. Telegraph poles had been torn out of the ground and flung down on the street, adding to the barricade of shattered roofs and walls.

Claus tied the reins and jumped down from the buggy.

The people of the town were crawling over the wrecked buildings like stunned ants. Some were clawing at the piles of lumber, trying to get to the source of cries and moans coming from under layers of broken buildings. Some were just walking around in a daze with blank expressions like sleepwalkers.

To his growing horror, Claus saw bodies everywhere. Some were lifeless. Some were writhing in pain and screaming for help. He saw one man clutching a plank that had gone through his abdomen like a spear. He saw a head severed from a body lying several yards away. He saw a child clutching a doll, both broken and still.

Frantically, he crawled over debris, hurrying to where his drugstore had stood. He was going to need a lot of chloroform and morphine.

At the Sontag place, Link Houston was frantically clearing away the lumber that had trapped Laura and her half brother and sister in the cellar. He'd dragged a section of wall off the pile and was able to hear Laura more clearly. He called to her, and she answered, but she couldn't seem to understand that it was Link calling to her. That made sense. She would think he was on the stage on the way to San Antonio.

Finally, he cleared his way to the cellar door. By then his hands were bleeding and pierced with splinters. He pulled the cellar door open. Three frightened faces looked up at him. Laura's eyes opened wide. "Link?" she asked, not believing what she saw.

"It's me," Link reassured her with a shaky grin.

Then she was out of the cellar and held tightly in his

arms. "Oh, Link," she sobbed. "I didn't think I'd ever see you again. But . . . but I saw them put you on the stage."

Link said, "The tornado hit the stagecoach a few miles from here, before it hit Endless. It knocked the stagecoach to smithereens. Killed everyone on it except me, I guess. I could see the tornado cloud was headed straight for Endless. I found a horse and got here as fast as I could."

He kissed her. The taste of her soft, trembling lips and the pressure of her firm, young curves against him sent a wave of emotions blazing through him. He felt a tenderness and caring for her and at the same time a powerful hunger for her sweet, young body. The feelings he had for her were stronger than any he'd had before in his life. He didn't ever want to let her go.

"I love you, Laura," he choked. "I was so scared for you. I was scared you'd got killed in the storm."

"I was scared, too," she said, clinging to him for strength, her legs weak and shaky. "The noise was terrible. I reckon being in the cellar saved us."

Paul and Ruth, their faces stained with tears, were hanging onto Laura's skirt. "It's okay, kids," she comforted them. "The mean old storm is over and we're all right."

The boy looked around, confused and bewildered. "But everything's gone—our house, the barn . . ."

"Just be glad you're all okay," Link told the boy. "Shucks, you can always get another house someplace."

Then a look of fright crossed Laura's face. "Father. He was in town, working on the church. Oh, Link . . ."

Paul and Ruth began crying again. "I want my Daddy," Ruth cried.

Link frowned. "I'm worried about my Pa, too. I reckon the storm hit his place as bad as any."

"We have to see about them," Laura said urgently. "We can go by your father's ranch house on the way into town to see about Elijah."

Link hesitated, looking worried. "I don't rightly know what I should do, Laura," he said. "I show my face in Endless, the sheriff is sure to grab me. I was hoping we could head out for Mexico. I love you, Laura. I want to start a whole new life with you. We could do that on the other side of the border. Please tell me you'll go with me. . . ."

Laura bit her lip, her eyes filling with tears. She looked searchingly into his eyes. "Link, I was never allowed to talk to you after you were arrested, but I couldn't believe you killed that man. Now I want to know. Please tell me the truth, Link."

"Laura, if you had your Bible here, I'd swear on it. I never killed nobody. The night of the killing, I was down at the border in a card game, but I couldn't prove it. Whoever killed Albert Milam is running around free, probably laughing because I was going to prison for what he done. If there's any justice in this life, he's got killed by the storm."

She looked deeply into his eyes and nodded soberly. "I can see you're telling me the truth. I knew in my heart you were innocent, but I just had to hear it from your lips. Now you've put my mind at rest. Link, I do want to go with you. I want to be with you. But I can't just go off someplace, not knowing if my father is hurt or needing me. I have to get into Endless to see about him.''

Link gazed at her, then looked in the direction of Endless, then at Laura again. ''Well, I don't know what to do. I keep thinking I ought to get away while I have a head start. But, when I look at you, Laura, I just can't think of anything except how beautiful you are and how bad I need you with me all the time. I never felt like that before. It keeps me from doing what my good sense tells me I ought to do.''

Laura pressed his hand against her tear-wet cheek. ''Oh, Link, I feel the same about you. I don't want you going to prison. I wanted to die after I saw them take you away on the stage, knowing I'd never see you again. Why don't you stay here while I go into town and see if my father needs me. I reckon the sheriff is going to be too busy with what's going on in town to be out lookin' for you.''

Link struggled with conflicting emotions. ''I can't let you go into Endless alone. Lord only knows what's going on there. Maybe folks will be so torn up by what happened they won't notice me. Anyway, let's go to my Dad's place first. If he's okay, he can help you get into town.''

Link tried to stand up. Under the grime and blood, his face turned pale. He swayed and sat down abruptly.

''Link! You're hurt!''

''It's my blamed leg,'' he said through clamped teeth. ''I reckon it's broke.''

"Let me see."

He pulled the leg of his Levi's up to his knee. The leg was swollen to the knee. The pressure felt as if it would split his boot apart.

"Oh, Link!" Laura gasped. "You've got to get that boot off and get to the doctor."

"First, we need to get to my Dad's place. I hope to God he's alive. We need somebody to look after you and the kids. I sure ain't much use with this bum leg."

"Don't worry about me," she said firmly. "I can look after myself. I'm strong and healthy. It's your hurt leg and my Pa and your Pa that's got me scared."

Laura's horse was nowhere to be found. The horse Link had ridden was able to carry him and Laura and Ruth. Paul trotted along beside them.

When they neared his home place, Link saw the damage was almost as bad as at the Sontag home. The fences were down, the big, comfortable ranch home his father had built out of adobe bricks was demolished. Only some of the walls were left standing. Half of the barn was gone.

Link felt a wave of relief when he saw his father limping around, poking at the rubble. The tough old Confederate vet had survived the storm. Link called to his father.

Ben Houston looked up. He frowned as Link rode into the yard with Laura and the children. He went on staring at Link, slowly shaking his head as if to clear it. When Link had come within a few yards, Ben could no longer question what he was seeing. He gasped Link's name.

"Yeah, it's me all right, Ben," Link said. "I reckon that

storm done me a big favor. The stagecoach got blown all to pieces. Far as I know, everyone on it was killed except me. The deputy was killed for sure. I got rid of the handcuffs and found this horse. . . ."

Ben shook his head. "I will be. . . . For a minute there I thought the storm had somehow scrambled my brains."

"Are you all right, Ben? Did you get hurt any?"

"I got banged around some. I'm sore all over, but nothing's broke." He looked ruefully at the remains of the house and barn. "Sure played the devil with the place, though. I never seen anything like it. Thought for a minute there I was in the middle of an artillery barrage at Gettysburg."

Then he turned his gaze to Laura on the horse in front of Link. How she came to be there was an intriguing question, but for the moment, he didn't ask. Instead, he said, "Miss Laura, I'm glad to see you lived through this god-awful thing."

"Thank you, Mr. Houston. We hid in the cellar and I guess that saved us," Laura said. "Link found us there and got us out."

She slid down from the horse and helped Link as he painfully dismounted. He would have collapsed if she hadn't been holding him. As she'd said, she was a strong young woman.

Ben asked, "Are you hurt?"

"It's my leg," Link said through clenched teeth.

"Let me see."

Houston knelt and shoved up Link's jean leg. He uttered

a shocked exclamation, then said, "Miss Laura, there's some hay in the part of the barn that's left standing. Let's get him over there."

"I can't stay around here," Link objected. "As soon as we see about Laura's daddy, I've got to light out for Mexico before the law catches up with me. Laura is going with me."

"You ain't likely to go anywhere with a leg like that, you darn fool," Ben growled. "You can't take this young girl across fifty miles of prairie in your condition. If the leg's broke, you could be dead with gangrene in less than a week. You'll be all right here for now. I'll be harboring a fugitive, but I reckon the sheriff's got his hands too full with what the storm done to the town to spend any time lookin' around for you."

With Laura helping, Ben got Link into the part of the barn that still had a roof. It was dry there. They eased Link down on a pile of soft straw.

Ben took out his pocket knife. He held it in his one hand and opened the blade with his teeth. "You'll need to help me some, Miss Laura," he said. "Link, you lie still now. I'll try not to hurt you any more than I have to."

He eased the razor-sharp blade under the top of the boot and slit the leather. Laura held the boot as Ben carefully cut it away.

Once, Link fainted from the pain. When his vision cleared, he was soaked with cold sweat and shivering so hard his teeth were chattering. Laura was holding his hand tightly. Tears were running down her cheeks.

The boot was off. His father looked at the leg, shaking his head. It was swollen twice its normal size and turning purple. "If I had both arms, I might could set it, but you'd probably go into shock from the pain and die. We need to get the doctor out here as soon as possible to take a look at it."

Then Ben uncorked a bottle and handed it to Link. "Take a swig of this whiskey. I found a couple of bottles that wasn't busted by the storm."

Link took several swallows of the liquor. Warmth spread through his body. He stopped shivering. Soon, the alcohol numbed some of the pain.

Laura sat beside Link, holding his hand. He looked up into her large, deep blue eyes that were fringed with long lashes. "I swear you're the prettiest thing this side of heaven, Laura. How come I got so lucky?"

"You hush and rest now, Link. I surely don't want to leave you, but I'll hurry back as soon as I find out how my father is, and we'll bring the doctor. I promise to get back real quick."

"Tell me you love me. I'll think about hearing you say it and that'll make the time go faster."

Her eyes looked long and deep into his. "Yes, I do love you, Link," she whispered. "I guess I love you very, very much."

"You're my sweetheart, right?"

Her cheeks flushed. "Yes, Link. I am your sweetheart."

Ben hitched a horse to his buckboard which miraculously had survived the storm. Then he came for Laura.

"C'mon, Miss Laura. Let's go see what's left of End-less."

Chapter Nine

With Laura beside him and the two children behind them in the wagon bed, Ben followed the road cautiously into town, picking his way around fallen trees and debris.

As they rode, Ben said, "I knew Link had taken a shine to you, Miss Laura, before he got in all his trouble over that killing. He talked about you. I reckon it's none of my business, but what I can't figure out is how the daughter of a preacher ever got sweet on that son of mine."

Laura looked down at her hands clasped in her lap. Her cheeks felt warm. "I don't think I can rightly explain it, Mr. Houston. I saw Link in town one day. He come up and spoke to me when I was in the general store. Something happened inside me. I . . . I felt like I'd fallen into sin, the kind of feelings he could stir up in me. I did a whole lot of praying, thinking I was wicked for having those kind of feelings. My Pa warned me not to talk to Link. I tried hard to stay away from Link, but I didn't have the strength. I disobeyed my father and I guess that was a sin, too. I slipped out at night so Link could come calling on me. It just didn't rightly seem to be a sin when I was with Link. It seemed the most natural and right thing in the world for us to be together, like God planned it that way.''

"Yeah, well, I can see why Link would have that effect on you," Ben said. "He's got more good looks than he needs. He's got a way with words. He could charm a Comanche into giving him his bow and arrow. I reckon you should have listened to your Pa, though. Link is my son, but you're lettin' yourself in for a whole bushel of misery getting tangled up with him. He's got a way of attracting trouble the way honey attracts flies. Now he's a fugitive from the law.''

"Mr. Houston, you're wasting your breath if you're trying to discourage me from being with Link," Laura told him, her blue eyes flashing.

"Yeah, I reckon I am," Ben muttered. "Nobody never yet talked any sense into young people who think they're in love.''

"I don't *think* I love Link. I *know*," Laura said angrily.

Ben chuckled. "Got a lot of spunk, ain't you? Well, it's your life. I just hate to see a decent young lady like you gettin' your life messed up. When Link come back home a few months ago, I had hopes maybe he'd changed. I was beginning to have some hopes that his life was going to straighten out at last. Next thing I knew, he was in trouble again. This time big trouble—charged with murder.''

"He had nothing to do with that killing," Laura said firmly, raising her chin. "Link swore to me he wasn't even in Endless that night. I truly believe him. I'm praying they find out who really killed that banker.''

"I hope your prayers get answered," said Ben, without conviction.

"Thank you, Mr. Houston. Right now, I'm busy praying inside that my Pa didn't get killed by the storm.''

They fell silent as the wagon brought them closer to Endless.

On the outskirts of town, they met with an incredible sight. Atop the wreckage of a house beside the road, illuminated by a pale shaft of the late afternoon's dying sun, sat a scarecrow-thin man playing a fiddle with all the energy in his frail body.

He paused to wave at them, fiddle in one hand, bow in the other, giving them a toothless grin. "Praise the Lord, I saved my fiddle!" he called out to them. "Lost everything else, but found my fiddle without a scratch on it.''

"Glad to hear that, Joe," Ben called back. "You go right on playing that fiddle.''

Ben muttered, "Crazy old coot. Fiddles while the town blows away like that Roman emperor that fiddled while Rome burned.''

No one could say for sure if Fiddling Joe was actually crazy, though he suffered from epileptic seizures. He claimed that he could make prophecies from visions he saw when having his seizures. Some believed it and went to him to see what the future held for them. One thing everyone agreed on was that Joe was a fiddling fool.

Nobody knew for sure what his last name was. He gave several, changing them from time to time, so the town settled on just calling him Fiddling Joe. He'd ridden into town one day five years ago, half starved and nearly dead of thirst. Nobody knew where he came from. He'd become a town fixture, playing his fiddle for square dances, weddings, funerals, and Fourth of July picnics. When he got going strong, the sounds he could coax from his fiddle could raise the hair on the back of a man's neck. The melodies he played were not of this world.

"I knowed the storm was comin'," he called after them. "I seen it in a vision two days ago. The devil's comin' to Endless to pay us all a visit. The storm was just his messenger to let us know he's on his way." Then he grinned, put his fiddle under his chin and began playing one of his eerie melodies.

"Good Lord, it looks like the devil's already been here," Ben gasped as they came closer into the town and saw the ghastly destruction and heard the cries of distress. He hadn't seen so much destruction and human suffering since the war.

When they came to the ruins of the church, Laura turned pale. She uttered a cry of anguish, quickly jumped down from the buckboard and knelt beside the still figure lying in the muddy churchyard amidst the wreckage.

The children crawled out of the wagon and ran after

Laura. Ben clambered down and joined them. Laura looked up at them. "Is he dead?" she asked in a choked voice.

Ben knelt beside her. He felt Elijah's wrist. "He's got a good, strong pulse."

"But he's so still." She cradled Elijah's head in her lap, making an attempt to wipe some of the mud from his face. Paul and Ruth stood beside her, both of them crying.

Laura said, "I don't know what to do for him. Can we get the doctor?"

Ben gazed down the road at the remains of the town scattered all over the prairie. He shook his head. "Lord, child," he muttered, "I don't know if the doctor is still alive. I'll go see what I can find out."

Ben was gone for an hour. When he returned, he was carrying a lantern, a blanket, and a large piece of canvas. "Looks like we might get more rain tonight," he told Laura. "Figured we could rig up some kind of shelter for your Pa. I found this stuff at what's left of the general store. I found the doctor, too. He's gonna come take a look at your Pa as soon as he can. He's trying to take care of an awful lot of people that are bad hurt."

It was after dark before Doctor von Blucher came to the church yard. The strain of the past hours was etched deeply in the lines of his face.

By then Elijah had regained partial consciousness, but he was rambling incoherently. Laura and Ben had erected a makeshift tent over him with the canvas. Laura had wrapped the blanket around him.

The young German doctor examined him by lamplight.

He told Laura, "I don't think he has any broken bones. Something hit the back of his head. So now his mind is confused. The best you can do for him is keep him warm and quiet. You shouldn't try to move him anywhere or let him stand up until his mind clears. I think by tomorrow he gets better."

After the doctor had examined Elijah, Ben called him aside. "Doctor, my son is out at my place with a hurt leg. It may be broken. He's in a lot of pain. How soon do you think you could get out to see him?"

"Ah, Herr Houston," the doctor said sadly, shaking his head, "*Gott in Himmel* only knows. Maybe in a day or two. There are so many people hurt. . . ." He made a helpless gesture toward the town. "Maybe a hundred or more."

Then Claus von Blucher took a small bottle from his bag. "Laudanum," he said, handing it to Ben. "It will ease some of the pain if your son suffers. It is all I can spare. We need so much here. I have sent a man to San Antonio for more medicine, but it will be two, three days before he gets back. Keep your son quiet, in the bed. I come as soon as I can."

Ben got Laura and her father as comfortable as possible under the makeshift tent. Then he said, "Guess I'll go on back to the ranch and see about Link."

Laura put her hand on Ben's arm. "Tell Link I'm thinkin' about him every minute. I'm just torn between wanting to be with him and needing to look after my Pa."

"I'll tell Link," Ben promised her. "But you're doing what's right to stay here with your Pa, Laura. Out of his head the way he is, he's liable to wander off someplace and hurt himself. Link will be okay.''

Ben tried to sound convincing, but he knew better. He knew if Link didn't get medical attention soon, he would lose the leg or die.

When he was back at his ranch, Ben found a lantern and hung it on a post near the hay where Link was lying. ''How's it going?'' he asked gruffly.

''I guess I've had better days,'' Link said. His face was gray with pain and fatigue.

''The doctor in town gave me this bottle of laudanum. It will ease the pain and let you get some rest.''

''Is Laura all right?''

Ben nodded. ''She said to tell you she's thinking about you every minute. The preacher got banged on the head. He's actin' kind of goofy. She needs to stay with him tonight to keep him from wandering around and hurting himself. Doctor said he ought to be all right by tomorrow.''

''Thanks, Ben. How soon can the doctor fix this blamed leg?''

Ben stretched the truth. ''Probably tomorrow. Lots of folks in town got hurt bad. He needs to take care of them tonight. I don't think I've the words to describe how bad things are in town. That tornado hit Endless square on. Every building is knocked flat or damaged. There are hurt and dead everywhere. Looks like towns I saw in the war after the Yankees got through shelling them.''

''Did you see the sheriff? Has he found out I wasn't killed when the storm hit the stagecoach?''

"Well, I reckon that's one thing you don't have to worry about for a while. There ain't no law in Endless. Sheriff Matt Blake and his deputy are both dead. All the telegraph lines are down. Endless is completely cut off from the rest of the world."

Chapter Ten

Ben waited until the laudanum had eased Link's pain. Then he said, "I have to get back to town to do what I can to help. There's still people trapped under some of those buildings."

Link nodded. The mixture of opium and alcohol in the medication took effect. He drifted off to sleep.

Ben unhitched his horse from the buckboard and saddled him. He could make better time on horseback.

The main street of Endless was a scene out of a bad dream. Lanterns, like fireflies, moved around, casting their pale lights on the wreckage. From beneath mounds of lumber came moans and cries of trapped victims. Rescuers dug frantically, trying to reach them. Ben Houston helped as much as he could with his one strong arm. Bodies of the dead were carried to a vacant field behind what had been the livery stable and laid in rows.

By then it had started to rain again, a steady downpour, soaking men to the skin, falling on the faces of the dead.

The injured were laid under as much shelter as could be rigged with sheets of canvas and tents.

Dr. Claus von Blucher wondered wryly what his colleagues in the modern operating rooms in Europe would think if they could see him now, setting broken limbs and operating by lantern light under a dripping canvas shelter.

Some men worked doggedly through the night, searching through the wreckage for bodies, dead and alive. Others wandered around with dazed expressions or just sat, staring at nothing. The cries and sobbing of family members crouched beside their dead loved ones in the open field mingled with the moans of the injured.

As a final touch to the nightmarish scene, all through the night could be heard far off in the distance the eerie strains of crazy Joe's fiddle.

The looting started before dawn.

Will Mariott, publisher of the weekly *Endless Gazette*, had saved his life during the storm by taking refuge under his Washington handpress. He had spent the night digging out the press from under boards and debris and collecting scattered type. The roof of his one-room newspaper building was gone. He covered the handpress with canvas to protect it from the rain. He was in a hurry to get the press back in operation so he could print a broadside listing the names of the tornado's victims.

He heard the shots as the first bloody rays of dawn were spreading over the desolate scene. Mariott went out to the street to find out who was shooting. In the dim half-light, he saw Jeff Altman, one of the owners of the Altman Brothers General Store, standing on the boardwalk in front of the badly damaged store with a smoking shotgun in his hand.

Altman had caught a looter picking through the wreckage of the store. He'd fired in the air, but as the man ran off, the store owner yelled curses and warned that the next time he'd shoot to kill.

The afternoon before, when Sid Milam got to town shortly after the storm passed, his worst fears had been confirmed. His new brick bank building was in ruins. Somewhere under the pile of bricks and rubble was the bank safe containing the money of the bank's customers and his own cash, mostly in the form of gold coins. The bank teller, bruised and badly shaken, but alive, had assured him that he'd transferred all the money from the cash drawer to the safe before the tornado struck.

Now, Milam's task was to guard the fortune. He reacted with frightened shock when he learned the town's sheriff and deputy had been killed by the tornado. To his utter dismay, the town was completely without law. With the telegraph lines down, he couldn't send a wire for help.

Milam knew word would spread to the renegade bands of rustlers and the thugs along the border. When they heard about the destruction of Endless and there being no law here, they'd surely come to loot and plunder. The main target would be his bank.

Milam was convinced the town was under siege. He was uneasy about using any of his ranch hands to help him stand guard. They were for the most part drifters and a rowdy bunch. He didn't trust them any more than the outlaws who would be riding into Endless.

Sid was up all night, heavily armed, patrolling the area of the bank. His fears were confirmed when Jeff Altman scared off a looter at dawn.

The injured were too busy coping with their pain and trying to cling to life to worry about looters. Those who lost their homes were sunk in despair as they picked through the remnants of their homes, searching for personal treasures, daguerreotypes of loved ones, family Bibles, pieces of clothing, dishes, heirlooms.

In the field where the dead were laid out, men with shovels and picks were overwhelmed by the task of trying to dig a hundred and fifty graves. Walter Morley, the town undertaker, went around pleading with families of victims to understand that he had lost most of his equipment in the storm and that it was impossible for him to embalm that many bodies.

Carpenters looked with despair over the field of the dead and knew it would take them a week to build that many pine-board caskets.

This morning after the storm, along Main Street, the businessmen of Endless began the enormous task of putting their town back together. First, an effort was made to clear some of the debris from the main street so horses and wagons could pass. Merchants salvaged what belongings they could.

News that Endless had been hit by a tornado and was without any law spread quickly. The looters were not townsfolk. They wouldn't sink so low as to steal from friends and neighbors. For the most part, the looters were strangers drifting into town.

Sid Milam's fears grew as he saw an increasing number of scruffy individuals on the streets, most of them armed, riding in from the road to Laredo. They stopped on the outskirts of town at Mexican Joe's saloon, the least damaged of the town's saloons, to get liquored up. Sadie Davis, the madam whose girls had plied their trade at the Sunset Saloon, was too smart a businesswoman to pass up this new flood of customers.

The town rapidly took on the atmosphere of lawless anarchy. Some hell-raisers were just drunken cowboys having a good time with no sheriff around to curtail their fun. They rode down Main Street, whooping it up and firing their guns in the air. But others were in town to steal whatever they could. The merchants had armed themselves in an effort to protect what they had left.

Later that day, Sid Milam knew his bank was doomed when he caught sight of the Coulter brothers, James and Billy, riding down Main Street toward his bank. With them were two cousins, the Wilson twins. The Coulter brothers were well-known outlaws in the region with a price on their heads. They had held up more than one bank and stagecoach when they weren't rustling cattle. They hadn't come to town to drink Mexican Joe's liquor or patronize Sadie Davis's girls or engage in any petty looting. They were here for the big prize—Sid Milam's bank.

It was near sunset of that day when the rider came out of the west. He was silhouetted by the setting sun that formed a flaming, scarlet halo around him. His features were lost in shadows.

Chapter Eleven

The rider was accompanied by three men on horseback. One of the three was slung over his saddle and tied with ropes to keep him from sliding to the ground. He was dead.

The rider passed the outskirts of Endless, then drew back on his reins when the full view of the town came into his line of vision. For a long moment, he stared at what had been Endless, then nudged his horse and entered the town. He came to a wrecked house on the edge of town. A small man thin to the point of emaciation was sitting atop the wreckage sawing away on a fiddle. The rider called to him. The fiddler put down his instrument, showing toothless gums in a grin.

The rider asked, "What happened here?"

The fiddler said, "Tornado. Hit the town yesterday."

The rider moved on, into the town, going down Main Street.

"Go on," the fiddler called after him. "The town's expecting you." Then he tucked his instrument under his chin and drew a mournful melody from the strings.

As his horse trotted down Main Street, hooves splashing through puddles of rainwater, the rider looked at the damaged buildings, the crumbled adobe walls, the storefronts blown down, the buildings without roofs or windows.

Where the meat market had stood was now only a heaped-up pile of boards. The barbershop had lost its roof and one wall. While the newspaper building was mostly rubble, by some miracle the printing press had survived and stood upright in the debris. The front of the restaurant was gone, but the kitchen still functioned. The owners had set up a long counter on sawhorses on the boardwalk in front under some canvas and were dishing out soup and coffee for survivors who had no other source of food. Altman's General Store was badly wrecked. Not much was left of the Sunset Saloon. The livery stable was torn apart. The blacksmith shop had no roof. All that was left of the opera hall was the false front. The roof and the other three walls were gone. The sign, ENDLESS OPERA HOUSE, was dangling at a ninety-degree angle from the beams of the front porch roof.

The rider noted it all carefully, his face expressionless.

Then he heard gunfire at the far end of the street. Some of the merchants along the street stopped what they were doing and stood out on the walk, staring in the direction of Sid Milam's bank.

The rider motioned to his two companions and they followed his horse down the street to where the shooting was going on. The rider drew rein and took in the situation at a glance.

Hiding behind the crumbling walls of the bank was a lone man. Approaching the bank were two men on horseback. One of the men shouted, ''Throw down your guns and come on out, Sid. You ain't got a prayer.''

The rider immediately recognized the man attacking the bank. ''Jim Coulter,'' he called.

Coulter twisted around.

The rider swung a leg over his saddle horn, dropped to the ground, and drew his six-gun in one smooth motion. He shot James Coulter between the eyes. James's brother Billy, holding a rifle, yanked the reins of his horse to face their new assailant. The rider shot him through the heart before his brother's body had slid from the saddle.

One of the Coulter cousins appeared on a rooftop. The rider's companion shot him. He went cartwheeling off the roof, hitting the ground with a sodden ''thud.'' He didn't move.

The other cousin on horseback came from behind a building, spurring his horse frantically to get away. The rider took casual aim and shot him in the back. His arms flew up. He tumbled from the saddle. His left boot was caught in the stirrup. His horse galloped out of town dragging the body through the mud.

Behind the section of brick wall, Sid Milam had watched the gunplay with wide, frightened eyes. He had no idea who the stranger was who had rescued him from the Coulter band. In those first moments, he wasn't sure he'd been rescued. He feared this had been a shoot-out between two bands of outlaws and he was in an even worse predicament. But the rider who had shot the Coulter brothers called out, ''Are you the owner of the bank?''

Sid replied in a shaky voice that he was.

The rider dropped his pistol back in his holster and walked toward the bank, leading his horse. Sid took some heart. Surely if the rider planned to rob the bank, he wouldn't approach with his gun holstered like that.

''Where's Sheriff Matt Blake?'' the stranger asked. ''How come he let a bunch like the Coulters into his town?''

Sid took heart and ventured from behind the wall. ''Matt Blake and his deputy were both killed yesterday when the tornado hit.''

He was going to say more, but something in the cold, expressionless eyes of the rider stopped the words. Sid thought his eyes looked like frozen chunks of black coal.

''Now that gives us a problem,'' the rider said. ''I've got something for him.''

Sid swallowed hard. Something about this man made him uneasy. ''What would that be?''

The rider jerked a thumb toward the dead body lashed to the third horse behind him. ''Another from the Coulter clan. Alex Coulter, James and Billy's uncle. Sheriff Matt

Blake had a poster out on him.'' The rider took a paper from his shirt pocket, unfolded it and showed it to Sid. Rain spattered on a rough drawing of man's face and the words, ''Reward—Five Hundred Dollars, Dead or Alive.''

Sid looked at the paper, then at the rider. ''You . . . uh . . . must be a bounty hunter.''

''You could say that,'' the rider said with a nod. ''Now about our problem. I know when Matt offered a reward like that it sure wasn't coming out of his pocket. I'd say this money comes from the county and Endless is the county seat. Now I've brought this man in and I want my money.''

''Yes, well, as you can see, you've come at a bad time. I'm sure if the county has posted a reward for this man, it will be paid. It's just that this is a real bad time. We're not going to be able to conduct any county business until we can get back to something like normal.''

Sid squirmed as the stranger continued to give him a cold, unblinking stare. The man took a sack of tobacco from his shirt pocket and thoughtfully rolled a cigarette. ''Looks like you do have a problem, friend,'' he murmured. ''A town without any kind of law is asking for trouble.''

Sid took out a handkerchief and mopped away some of the cold perspiration that had beaded his brow during his confrontation with the Coulter brothers. ''We've got plenty of trouble, all right. Drunk cowboys shooting up the town. Looters. And you see what nearly happened here.'' Sid waved his hand at his bank building and the bodies in the street. ''I owe you a lot of thanks, stranger.''

The rider smiled coldly. ''You'll probably wind up owing me a lot more than that, friend. How about the sheriff job? Is it open?''

Sid looked at him in surprise. "Why I . . . I guess so. You mean you'd be interested?"

The stranger nodded slowly. "The bounty-hunting business hasn't been so good lately. You might say I already work with the law to some degree, hunting wanted men."

"Well, you sure know how to handle yourself in a gunfight," Milam agreed. "And we need protection. No question about that. Under normal circumstances, we'd have to hold an election, but this is an emergency. I can get the mayor to appoint a sheriff. At least until the town rebuilds and we can have a regular election. What's your name?"

"People call me different names. 'Smith' is okay."

By then a crowd was gathering around the scene of the shoot-out. Sid Milam saw the mayor, Ned Bradley, among them. Bradley operated a small real estate and insurance business in Endless. His office building on Main Street had been badly damaged like all the others.

Sid called Bradley aside, leading him off a short distance where they could talk. "Ned, this man, Smith, has asked for the job of sheriff until we can have a regular election. I think you ought to go ahead and appoint him. He's demonstrated how well he can handle himself with outlaws. With a man like that patrolling the streets I don't think we'd have to worry any more about looters. We'd be safe."
And so would my bank vault, Milam added to himself.

Bradley looked surprised. "Sid, we don't know anything

about this man. He might be as bad an outlaw as the Coulters.''

"He's a bounty hunter," Sid said impatiently. "Ned, if he was an outlaw, he could easily have shot the Coulters to get them out of the way, then gone ahead and robbed the bank, himself."

"I don't know," Bradley murmured, staring at the stranger. "The way he shot those Coulter brothers. And their cousin that was trying to get away. He cold-bloodedly shot the man in the back." Bradley shuddered. "He's got to be some kind of gunslinger."

"Well, shoot, Ned, so are most of the sheriffs in frontier towns. Bat Masterson, Wild Bill Hickok, Wyatt Earp— they're nothing but gunslingers who happen to be wearing a badge."

"Don't you think we need to hold an election . . .?"

Sid Milam was rapidly losing his temper. "Hold an election with the town in this condition? Just who around here do you think would want the job? There isn't a man in Endless who hasn't lost his business or his home or someone in his family. They're all going to be too busy burying their dead and trying to rebuild their homes and businesses. We're darn lucky a man like Smith came along. He's tough, fast with a gun. He'll get those rowdy cowpokes and drifters back in line and restore some law and order in Endless. Remember, Ned, it isn't only my money in the bank safe. Most of the merchants in town have money in that safe, and the county tax money is there, too.

If we don't get law protection in this town fast, there'll be more outlaws coming to rob that safe.''

Ned Bradley was a weak man. He liked being mayor and knew full well he couldn't get reelected without Sid Milam behind him. The storm had demoralized him even more. His home had been blown down. His wife had been hurt. He didn't give Sid any further argument. ''Whatever you think is best, Sid,'' he mumbled.

''Do you have Matt Blake's badge?''

''It's over in my office. Or what's left of my office,'' Bradley said ruefully.

''All right. Let's take this fellow Smith over there and swear him in right now. I think we're lucky he came along.''

Immediately after Smith was sworn in and given the sheriff's badge, he insisted on deputizing the two men who had ridden into town with him. They looked like a pair of cutthroats, but Sid Milam could see no problem with that. A good strong sheriff with two able deputies would restore badly needed law and order to Endless. ''All right,'' Sid agreed.

''You got a sign painter in the town?''

''Yes,'' Milam replied. ''Billy Joe Turner has a sign-painting business. His building got blown away in the storm, but I reckon he's got some paint and brushes left. What do you want with a sign painter?''

''I want two signs. I want one to say nobody can come into this town wearing a gun. On the other I want the words in big, red letters, 'LOOTERS WILL BE HANGED.' ''

"Good Lord, man," the mayor said, swallowing hard, "you can't just go around hanging people. You got to have a legal trial. . . ."

Smith gave him a black-eyed look that turned the blood frigid in Ned Bradley's veins. "Yes, I can," Smith said softly. "This is my town now."

Chapter Twelve

The next morning, Laura Sontag sat under the makeshift canvas tent, listening to the rain spattering on her shelter. It was Sunday. Sunlight could not penetrate the dark, sullen clouds. There were occasional flashes of lightning and the rumble of thunder. There was a chill in the air.

Since the tornado struck on Friday afternoon, Laura had been through experiences for which nothing in her life had prepared her. She felt heavily burdened down with grief and care and bone-tired from getting very little sleep. She was moving in a dreamworld that had lost all touch with reality as she had known it. The sight of so many dead people, a lot of them children, was not the kind of reality that her mind could accept. The surroundings that had been her familiar frame of reference, the buildings on Main

Street, the homes where people she knew lived, were gone
or had become grotesque wrecks. Nothing about her world
was familiar any more. She was in a foreign land.

Everything had changed, everything was strange, and
that included her father. Elijah had awakened the morning
after the storm, apparently all right physically except for a
headache. But there was something different about him. He
sat staring at his demolished church murmuring, "My God
is a God of vengeance," over and over. Then he'd gotten
up and gone staggering off in the rain to see about the
members of his congregation, to pray for the injured and
help bury the dead. Laura had seen very little of him since
then. When she did, it was like trying to talk to a stranger.
He appeared dazed, a sleepwalker, looking at her but not
really seeing her, listening to her words, but not understanding what she said.

That first day after the storm, Paul and Ruth were so
hungry they were crying. Laura's stomach cramped with
hunger. Then some people had come by to tell Laura about
the soup being given free by the owners of the restaurant,
and she got some for herself and her brother and sister.

Mostly, she stayed in the churchyard, under the makeshift tent. She was afraid to go down to Main Street. There
was often the sound of loud, angry voices, of horses, and
gunshots. She ventured down there only to get food from
the restaurant.

Link Houston was in her thoughts constantly. He was
part of the dream state that had overtaken her. Had he really
come back to free her and Paul and Ruth from the cellar

of their demolished home? Then she thought about his terrible injury, thought about him lying on the hay in his father's wrecked barn. When the doctor finally got to him would he have to take Link's leg off? Would Link die there on the hay in the barn? The thoughts she had about Link were terrible thoughts filled with despair. She had cried when they took Link away on the stage, when she thought she'd never see him again. And now she cried because she thought that, although he had come back, he might die.

Elijah's words echoed in her mind. "My God is a God of vengeance." Was that true? If it was, it was a terrifying thought. She had believed that God was like a kindly father, looking after her welfare. But where was He now when she was so frightened and people were hurt and dying all around?

She didn't fully understand what was happening to her life, and least of all, her feelings about Link Houston. She'd had no experience with those kind of feelings that involved a man. She was too young to have anything by which she could measure those feelings. She only knew that she was filled inside with an overwhelming tide of emotion when Link came into her mind. She longed for him as if a part of her was missing. When she was with him she was happy and when he touched her it made her glad all over. She wanted to do for him whatever would make him happy and she wanted to be very close to him.

She was so buried in her thoughts that she wasn't aware of the time passing. It was mid morning when a buckboard rattled into the cluttered churchyard. She looked up and recognized Link's father, Ben Houston.

She jumped up and ran out to the buckboard, unmindful of the rain. "How is Link?" she blurted out.

Ben stepped down from the wagon and led her back to the canvas shelter. "I just spoke with the doctor. He reckons he's finally going to find the time to ride out to the ranch to see to Link. I tell you, Miss Laura, this town sure owes its thanks to that doctor. The man hasn't slept or rested in forty-eight hours. He's been operating on folks, setting broken limbs and sewing up cuts since Friday afternoon. He's done what he could with the worst injured and now he's going to have a look at Link's broke leg."

Laura felt a surge of hope. "I'm so glad to hear that," she said fervently.

"Are you faring all right here?"

"I guess you could say so, besides being cold and hungry a lot."

"How is your father?"

"He 'pears to be all right. I mean, he's getting around all right, but he's acting kind of strange, like . . . well, like maybe he's a bit touched."

"I'd suspect a lot of folks around here are in that state of mind after what they've been through. Well, I guess I'll be getting back to my place. I probably ought to be there when Doctor von Blucher comes to set Link's leg."

"I want to go with you," Laura said immediately. "My father doesn't need me anymore. He's off somewhere, taking care of his church folk."

Ben frowned. ''Well, I ain't your Pa to tell you what to do, Miss Laura, but I already warned you about how you're askin' for trouble, gettin' involved with that no-account son of mine.''

''Mr. Houston, I reckon I can look out for myself. Since Friday, I was nearly killed by a tornado. My home got blown down. This church building that my father worked and prayed for all his life got smashed to pieces. I've seen dead folks lying in the street. I don't think there's much worse can happen to me. And, Mr. Houston, I don't mean no disrespect, but I'll thank you not to call Link 'no-account.' I know you'n him don't get along so well, but you shouldn't judge him so harshly.''

Ben gave her a hard look, then said wryly, ''Well, all I got to say is, you're a fine young lady and a lot better than Link deserves. I hope he appreciates you. But I reckon it would be best for you and your brother and sister to get away from here. There was a killing down at the bank late yesterday. Four men were gunned down. Right now, this town is no place for a young woman alone with two children. You'd be safer for a while out at my place.''

''I was thinking of leaving Paul and Ruth with Mrs. Anne Wallace. She loves them, and I'm sure she'd be real happy to have them stay with her.''

Ben nodded. ''We'll go right by Mrs. Wallace's place. We can leave them off there.''

Laura got her brother and sister who were playing on the other side of the wrecked church building. They all climbed on the buckboard and Ben slapped the reins on the back of his horse.

On the way to his ranch, Ben pulled off on a side road and stopped at the home of Anne Wallace, a widow who often kept the children. Her house had not been in the path of the tornado, so was relatively undamaged.

The woman welcomed the children with open arms. Then she looked with dismay at Laura whose dress was torn and muddy. "You poor child. Don't you have any other clothes?"

Laura was embarrassed. "I know I look a sight, Mrs. Wallace, but everything I owned was blown away by the storm."

"Well, you can't go around in those rags. The only thing I have are some shirts and Levi's that belonged to my husband. They'll be too big for you, but it's the best I can do for you until I can sew you some dresses."

A lump filled Laura's throat. "You're so good to us, Mrs. Wallace."

"Oh, shucks. Far as I'm concerned, you and your brother and sister are family."

Laura changed into the shirt and Levi's Mrs. Wallace offered her. By rolling up the shirtsleeves and the cuffs of the Levi's, Laura was able to wear them. It felt good to be in clean, dry clothes, even if they didn't fit.

Then they went on to the Houston ranch.

When Laura saw Link, pale from the pain in his swollen leg, her heart came up in her throat, choking her. It was hard, seeing him like this. She wanted to will his leg to heal, to have him standing tall and strong again, the way he should be.

Link managed a shaky smile and tried to sit up. "Gee, it's good to see you, Laura." In spite of his pain, there was joy in his eyes at the sight of her.

She felt the same joy. She sat on the hay beside him, holding his hand tightly. She blinked back tears. "You lay back down now, Link. The doctor's coming to fix your leg."

"That right?" Link looked at his father for confirmation.

Ben nodded. "I talked to him early this morning. He's done with the worst of his operations, so he's coming out in a little while."

Ben avoided looking at Link's swollen leg. He was wondering if it was already too late to save the leg.

"What if he tells folks in town that I'm here?" Link asked anxiously.

"He ain't gonna tell anybody," Ben said impatiently. "I told him all about how the tornado hit the stagecoach and you made it all the way back here with that hurt leg. He's the kind of man who is just concerned about taking care of the sick. He stays out of the private lives of his patients and lets the law take care of its own matters."

Sensing that Link wished he could be alone with Laura, Ben went outside.

Laura sat close to Link on the hay, remembering the nights she had slipped out to meet him and the time she had cuddled in his arms in the hay of her father's barn, feeling safe and warm as they listened to the rain spattering on the roof. Now she tried to recapture that good feeling. Link talked about how things were going to be for them as soon as his leg was better. He talked about a new life for them in Mexico, where they would get married and be together and raise a family. Laura wanted to believe everything he was telling her, but she was filled with a dark sense of foreboding. She feared that the tornado had brought some kind of evil to Endless and it was going to infect all of their lives.

Within an hour, Doctor von Blucher drove his buggy into the yard. He got his bag of medical supplies and wearily followed Ben to the barn.

"So, Link, how are you feeling?" he asked when he entered the barn.

"Not like going to a square dance."

"No, I think not," the doctor said. He put down his bag and knelt beside Link. He spent several minutes examining the leg, probing and twisting gently. "Sorry I hurt you," he apologized, "but this I must do."

When he had completed his examination, he said, "So now we give some chloroform and you sleep a little while I set the broken bone."

With Laura and Ben helping, he administered the chloroform, dripping it on a cone placed over Link's face. When he was satisfied that Link was unconscious, he set the broken bone back in place. Then he mixed up a plaster solution and formed a cast that encased the lower leg and foot.

When the procedure was completed and Link was groggily coming awake, Ben followed the doctor back to his buggy.

"We wait and see," Dr. von Blucher told Ben. "If the gangrene comes, we have to take the leg off. We know in a few days. Keep him quiet until the plaster is hard. The cast must stay on for five or six weeks."

The doctor stepped up into his buggy seat. He picked up the reins, then paused to add, "Ben, the lawyer, Victor Crenshaw, was hurt very much in the storm. There is nothing I can do for him. I think he lives not more than a few more hours. He keeps saying he wants to talk to you. It seems of great importance to him. I think you must go soon if you see him before he dies."

"What in tarnation does he want to see me about?"

The doctor shrugged. "*Ich weiss nicht.* I don't know. I only know he begs to see you."

"Well, then I reckon if the man's dying, I ought to go."

With Laura there to take care of Link, Ben knew he was not needed and probably not wanted. He hitched up his buckboard and rode back into town to see Victor Crenshaw and get some supplies.

Having the doctor treat Link's leg was one concern off Ben's mind, but he had another equally serious. Late yesterday, the mayor at Sid Milam's urging had appointed a new sheriff. Ben hadn't witnessed the shooting at the bank, but he'd heard all about it. This new sheriff was a bounty hunter and a cold-blooded killer. The description given by those who had seen this stranger was chilling. If he found out Link had survived the tornado and started looking for him, it would be serious. And Link was in no shape to ride fifty miles to the Mexican border.

Ben found Victor Crenshaw on a cot under one of the tents that had been set up for the seriously injured. He looked so still and lifeless that Ben thought he was already dead. But when Ben sat beside the cot and spoke his name, Crenshaw's eyes fluttered open.

"Oh, Ben. I'm so glad you came," he said weakly. "Could you help me sit up, please?"

"Sure."

Crenshaw was clutching a bottle of whiskey. When Ben got him elevated to a half-sitting position, he gulped some of the liquor. A bit of color came back to his gray cheeks. Ben gently laid him back down.

The lawyer had a coughing spell that wracked his body. He wiped blood from his lips with his sleeve. "Doc can't do anything for me," he whispered hoarsely. "Chest all caved in." Then he grasped Ben's arm urgently. "Ben, I had to talk to you. I don't want to die with your boy's life on my conscience. Link did not kill Albert Milam."

"Well, I hope that's true, Victor."

"Ben, I didn't do right by your boy." Tears trickled down the old lawyer's cheeks. "I never was much of a lawyer. If Link would have had decent legal council, he'd be a free man. I let him down real bad. I just never was any good in a courtroom. Ben, I want to beg your forgiveness."

"Victor, you don't have to do that. I know you done the best you could . . ."

"Listen," Crenshaw said urgently, clutching at Ben's sleeve. "There was something wrong about that trial. I think somebody bribed one or more of those jurors to give a verdict that saved Link from a hanging."

Ben looked at him with surprise. "I guess it's possible that somebody paid that drunk, Walt Sawyer, to claim he saw Link leave Albert Milam's office the night of the shooting. But why would somebody pay a person on the jury *not* to hang Link? That just plain doesn't make sense."

"I know. But Ben, the whole town was in a hanging mood after the banker was murdered. You know that. I put up such a weak defense for Link, there was no reason for the jury not to have him hung. But they didn't do it. They were out for two days, then came back with the verdict of a less serious crime. There's something wrong about that."

Crenshaw had another coughing spell. He closed his eyes, gasping for breath. When he could speak, he said, "Ben, you need to find out which ones held out for a voluntary manslaughter verdict. Talk to the jury foreman, Caster Lambert. I wanted to do it, but I was afraid to. I'm a coward, Ben. I was afraid if I got to poking around, asking too many questions, I'd get a bullet through my brain. Something was going on about that murder that nobody has even come close to guessing. Ben, if you can find out who bribed the jury and why, you could clear Link and get him set free."

He began coughing again and drifted into a coma. An hour later, Victor Crenshaw died.

Ben left the tent. He stood on the boardwalk looking up

and down Main Street. Endless was rapidly becoming a tent city. Several merchants had set up tents beside their damaged buildings, putting their merchandise and belongings under canvas, out of the rain, until they could get their buildings repaired.

Altman Brothers General Store had suffered severe damage. The roof was gone and one entire wall had collapsed. Much of the goods in the store was buried under piles of rubble. Still, the Altman brothers were doggedly open for business, knowing they had supplies—tents, lanterns, axes—desperately needed by the town. They had set up a cash register on the boardwalk in front of the store. Customers were invited to hunt through the wreckage. If they found anything they needed, they brought it to the cash register and paid for it. At night, the brothers took turns guarding against looters.

Ben picked his way through the debris-filled aisles of the ruined store. He gathered what he could find of food supplies that were not ruined: lard, coffee, bacon, some canned peaches. Under a piece of roofing tin, he found a bag of flour miraculously protected from the rain. In one corner, under a pile of rubble, he made a lucky find for Link—a pair of crutches. Nearby, he found three army cots.

When Ben was paying for the supplies, Jeff Altman, who was manning the cash register, gave him a curious look as he rang up the price of the crutches and the cots. "You got company, Ben?"

Houston made a feeble excuse about getting the cots and the crutches for a neighbor, but the store owner followed him with a curious gaze as Ben loaded the supplies into his buckboard. Altman's curiosity made Ben uneasy. Sooner or later, the people in town were going to find out that Link was not among those killed in the stagecoach. Would they send the sheriff to his place, looking for Link?

When he returned to the ranch, Ben built a campfire. Laura made biscuits, fried bacon, and boiled coffee. They ate the meal in the shelter of the damaged barn beside Link's bed of hay.

Ben told Link about Victor Crenshaw's dying words.

Link gave his father a searching look. "Do you think he was onto something, Ben? That business about the jury being bribed?"

"I don't put much stock in it," Ben said. "Old Victor was pretty senile. Maybe it was just a crazy notion he got in his head."

Link thought for a moment. "It doesn't make much sense," he admitted. "Why would the killer go bribe the jury *not* to have me hanged? Seems like he'd want me hanged. That would settle the matter and the killer would be safe."

Ben agreed. Then he said, "On the other hand, I got to admit it does seem mighty peculiar that the jury decided on a verdict that would result in a jail sentence instead of a hanging. The whole town wanted you hanged."

Laura suggested, "Maybe whoever done the killing got to feeling so wicked, sending an innocent man to the gallows, that they paid the jury to give a lighter sentence."

"Could be, I guess," Ben said. "Hardly seems likely, though."

Link fell silent. He thought about the day Albert Milam was killed. He had gone to Milam's office early in the afternoon to try and talk the banker into extending the time on his father's lease. Link had pleaded with Milam to give his father a chance. Albert Milam had been insolent and arrogant. Words became heated. Milam ordered him out of his office. Link's temper exploded. He knocked the pompous banker down. Several people in the bank including the bank teller, Jake Simms, heard the argument. They stared at Link as he stormed out of the bank. They later testified at the trial that there was bad blood between Link and the murdered man. The teller, Simms, testified that he'd rushed into Albert Milam's office after the fight and helped the banker to his feet. Simms also said he'd heard Link warn Albert Milam that he was going to kill him. That, Link knew, was a lie. He'd made no such threat.

Link had ridden out of town and gotten in the all-night poker game in a little town near the border. When he returned to Endless the next day, he learned that Albert Milam had been shot to death at the bank late the night before and the sheriff was looking for Link. Somebody else in Endless had shot Albert Milam to death in his office at the bank that night. But who? Who in Endless had it in for the banker enough to shoot him in cold blood?

Ben interrupted Link's thoughts. "There's something else I need to tell you. Endless has a new sheriff."

Link gave his father a startled look. "Already? Who is it?"

"A stranger. A guy named Smith. Rode into town from God knows where late yesterday. A real cold-blooded gunslinger. He no sooner got into town than he got in a shootout with the Coulter brothers who were trying to rob Sid Milam's bank. Killed them both and their two cousins. Said he was working as a bounty hunter. Sid Milam is running scared that in a town without law, sooner or later his bank is going to get robbed. So, he talked the mayor into appointing this Smith fellow sheriff until Endless recovers enough to have an election. With a man like that wearing a badge it might be smart for you to get across the Rio Grande into Mexico just as soon as your leg is well enough for you to travel."

"Yeah, but how long will that be? I can't ride a horse or take care of Laura crippled up like this."

"Maybe we could take you there in the wagon."

Link was thoughtful again. "Y'know, Ben, that's what I've been doing all my life. Hightailing it to save my hide every time things got rough. If I take Laura and we run off to Mexico, we'll spend the rest of our lives on the run with this murder hanging over me. I owe it to Laura to give her a better life than that. You think we could talk to some of the folks that were on that jury before that new sheriff comes lookin' for me? Maybe there's something to what Victor Crenshaw said. Maybe we could find out who really killed Albert Milam."

"That's takin' a big chance," Ben grumbled. "I'll give

you credit for not running away from trouble for a change, like you usually do. But this is one time you might be smart to leave. I sure wouldn't want that new sheriff coming around looking for me. They say there's something about that man that ain't natural.''

Chapter Thirteen

The hanging took place the next morning shortly after dawn. The body dangled from the rope tied from the eaves of the damaged porch of the opera house. There had been a brilliant flash of lightning and clap of thunder when Smith slapped the rump of the horse and it ran from under the condemned man. He had jerked and kicked in his death struggle for a few minutes, then hung there in the rain, turning slowly in gusts of wind that swept down Main Street, flapping the canvas tent flaps.

On the shirt of the executed man was pinned the sign, THIS IS WHAT HAPPENS TO LOOTERS.

Just before the hanging took place, a crowd of people had gathered in the street, standing in the rain, filled with horror at what they were about to see. Milton Dickson, the

115

owner of the restaurant, had pleaded desperately with the new sheriff. "It's just old Juan Cardoza. Everybody in town knows him. He's got a big family. He was just trying to get something for his children to eat. I don't want the man hung."

Smith asked, "Did you tell this man he could sneak into your place of business before dawn and help himself to your food supplies?"

"Well, no. It's true he was stealing, but if a man's family is hungry and he takes a little food, that ain't no hanging offense."

"We have a serious situation in this town. You can't have law and order until you stop this looting," Smith said coldly.

"I'm not going to stand here and see that poor man hung," Dickson had shouted frantically.

Smith, astride his big stallion, looked down at Dickson with hard, black eyes. Quietly, dangerously, he asked, "Do you want to stop me?"

Dickson stared up at Smith's eyes black as hard coal and then saw his right gloved hand moving toward his Colt revolver. He had witnessed the shoot-out at Sid Milam's bank late Saturday, had seen Smith draw his gun faster than the eye could follow. He felt a cold chill run through his body.

The restaurant owner stood shivering in the rain, watching helplessly as Smith put the rope around the neck of the sobbing old man, then slapped the rump of the horse on which he was seated. Dickson watched the old man's death struggle, saw his kicking feet, his bulging eyes, his swollen tongue. Then he stumbled away to the side of a building, and was violently sick.

After Smith had pinned the sign to the dead man's shirt. He told the watching crowd, ''Spread the word around what you just saw. Let the looters know what's waiting for them here.''

Will Mariott had watched the event, then, filled with rage, he had walked up Main Street to his ruined newspaper building. Since the storm, he had erected a makeshift roof of tin and canvas over his printing shop. He had cleaned his press and had dug boxes of type out of the storm's debris. He angrily composed a one-page editorial as he hand-set the type, dropping it letter by letter in the tray.

He had several dozen copies printed by noon. With the ink barely dry, he started down Main Street, handing a copy to every person he encountered.

A few hours later, a dozen of the town's leading citizens crowded into the mayor's damaged office building. Anger boiled in the air. Milton Dickson demanded, ''What kind of monster have you turned loose on us, Ned?''

The mayor was seated behind his desk, which was still cluttered with debris from the storm. He looked around uncomfortably at the sullen group. ''Wh . . . what do you mean, Milton?''

''You know full well what he means, Ned Bradley,'' Will Mariott exclaimed. ''He's talking about that ruthless gunslinger you appointed sheriff.''

''The man's a cold-blooded killer,'' Milton Dickson exclaimed. He spread his hands on the desk and leaned toward Bradley. "You know he lynched poor old Juan Cardoza. He caught old Juan stealing from my restaurant, took him right down and lynched him. No trial. No judge. No jury. It was my restaurant. My food Juan stole. I told Smith I didn't want that poor old man hung. I said I wasn't pressing charges. He went right ahead with the hanging. I think he enjoyed it. Juan's body is still hanging down there. His wife and children are standing there, begging for somebody to take the body down. How do you think they feel? One of Smith's deputies is guarding the place. Won't let nobody go near the body."

Suddenly a voice from the doorway interrupted. "We're facing a desperate situation in this town, Milton. With no law, we're at the mercy of looters and outlaws. It's a time that calls for strong measures."

The men turned. Sid Milam was standing in the doorway. He moved into the crowded room. He held out a copy of Will Mariott's one-page newspaper. "That's awful strong language you used in your paper, Will. You called Smith some slanderous names. The man is just doing the job we hired him to do—bring some law and order back to Endless."

"It's too big a price, Sid," the newspaper publisher said. "You have to get rid of that man."

"That's what you said here," Sid Milam said, pointing to the paper. "You're getting these folks all riled up, and that's bad, Will. We need to put this town back together. We can't do it with outlaws roaming our streets. We need protection for our homes and businesses. We need law and order.''

"Sure we need law and order, Mr. Milam," Will Mariott said, "but I don't call lynching a man without a trial law and order. Your man Smith has the whole town scared of him.''

"A good lawman needs that kind of respect," Milam said. "You've noticed there aren't any more drunk cowboys riding down Main Street, shooting their guns in the air. Smith has a tent set up on the edge of town next to Mexican Joe's saloon. Anybody riding into town has got to check his guns with one of the deputies there. And I'm sure after seeing Juan Cardoza's body hanging from the opera house eaves, looters are gonna think twice.''

Milam continued, "If it hadn't been for Smith, the Coulter brothers would have cleaned out my bank vault Saturday afternoon. We need to protect the bank. The future of this town depends on it. All you folks with business that got hit by the tornado are going to need capital to rebuild. Where will you get it? I'll tell you. You'll need to get loans from the bank. How're you going to do that if we don't have a strong sheriff to keep outlaws like the Coulter family from coming into town and cleaning out the bank safe?

"Jeff Altman, how are you and your brother going to rebuild your general store? I happen to know you've given credit to every rancher in the county because of the drought. You're strapped for cash. It's the same with almost every merchant in town. Now, I'm promising every man here a loan from my bank. But stop this talk about running off our new sheriff.''

"Well, maybe you got a point, Sid," Jeff Altman mumbled. "None of us like the man, but at a time like this maybe you got to fight fire with fire."

Some of the other merchants reluctantly agreed and began moving toward the doorway.

Will Mariott remained firm. "Smith was not elected by the people in this town, Sid. You and the mayor just took it on yourself to appoint him. You didn't even ask the city council. I'm a member of the council. If I get the other council members to agree, we're going to take the man's badge.''

Sid Milam gave him a cold smile. "Go ahead, Will. But I think the man that tries to take Smith's badge had better get himself a coffin built first.''

Late that afternoon, Smith and his two deputies rode up to Will Mariott's newspaper building. They tied their horses to the hitch rail and entered the ruined building.

The newspaper publisher was setting type for a follow-up edition condemning the new sheriff's brutality and demanding his resignation. "Who is this man, Smith?" his editorial asked. "What do we know about him? Where does he come from? How do we know he doesn't have a price on his head?''

Under the sullen, black clouds, it had already grown dark. Rain was drumming on the makeshift roof of canvas and tin. Mariott was setting type by lamplight. Hearing the men walk in, he looked up.

Smith came in with his deputies following. He was holding one of the papers Will Mariott had distributed earlier. It was soggy from the rain. Smith's face was hard and angry.

"You called me some mighty bad names in your paper, Mister. Care to repeat them to my face?"

"Surely," Will Mariott said, facing the tall man. "I said you were a psychopathic killer, that you had no business wearing a badge, and that the citizens of Endless should take your badge back and run you out of town . . ."

Smith slapped the newspaper publisher so hard the blow knocked the smaller man against the wall. Then he nodded to his deputies. They were both carrying axes. They went to work, systematically smashing the Washington press.

"No!" Will cried. He tried to stop them. Smith drew his gun and pistol-whipped the newspaper publisher across the room. With blood running down his face, Mariott slammed against a wall and slid to the floor.

When the press was battered beyond use, Smith had his deputies drag Mariott over to the press. They tied him over the ruined press.

"I ought to kill you," Smith said in a cold, deadly voice. "No man has ever called me the kind of names you printed in your paper and lived to talk about it. But I want you to live and tell the rest of the town what to expect if they try to keep me from doing my job here."

Then he turned to one of the deputies. "Jesse, you want to have some more fun with this man?"

The swarthy deputy looked at the bound publisher and grinned wickedly.

Smith grabbed Mariott's hair, lifting his blood-streaked head to face him. "Jesse here likes to hear men cry and beg for mercy. We need to keep Jesse happy, don't we?"

The two deputies bound Marriot to the ruined press. Then Smith and his second deputy went outside and untied their horses. As they were riding away, Smith heard Will Mariott's scream.

Elijah Sontag stood in the churchyard, staring at the pile of broken boards that a few days ago had been his beautiful church. It was late afternoon, but turning dark with the sun lost behind black, roiling clouds. Several times in the past three days, he had come here to stand and look at the wrecked building. Now the rain was coming down hard, plastering his hair, streaking his face, soaking his clothes. He was not aware of his physical discomfort. The pain in his soul was too great.

When he had regained consciousness the morning after the storm, his head was hammering with pain. He was befuddled, half dazed. He numbly understood that some evil force had destroyed his church. He had gone stumbling off, driven by knowing in some kind of dumb, instinctive way, that there were people who needed him.

He had sat beside the cots of the hurt and dying, repeating the words expected of him. Somebody had given him a Bible. He held it while he said the words. He had stood in the rain beside sobbing parents as their children were buried in the muddy earth and again said the words out of habit. His heart had wrenched with agony at the grief of these poor people. These were children he had baptized, had taught in Sunday school.

Now it was late Monday. It all ran together in his throbbing mind, the moans of the injured, the sight of ruined buildings and houses, the bereaved kneeling in the mud beside their dead loved ones. His head throbbed and hurt. Something in his brain felt as if it would explode.

He stared at the ruined church. He realized he was still clutching the Bible, so wet now it was just a soggy lump.

"You are a wrathful God," he mumbled, looking at the pile of boards. He could see the battered remains of the altar his parishioner had lovingly made.

All of his life, he had tried to understand the nature of evil. He could understand the nature of good. God was good. He was a loving father, who forgave and comforted. Elijah could understand that. But how to explain evil? He had thought evil came about as something man brought on himself by his sinful nature. Until now that had satisfied him, even when his first and second wife died. They had been taken from him because of his inherent sinful nature. He had not prayed diligently enough, had not done enough for other people, had violated the laws of God, so it was just that he pay the price.

Yes, but now he was faced with a situation that confounded all of his theology. Surely the town of Endless had not been so evil that it had to suffer the fate of Sodom and Gomorrah. Had the little children he'd seen buried in muddy graves been that evil? Had God sent the tornado to wipe out the town because it was that bad? He had trouble believing that. It was an ordinary small town with good, hard-working people, most of whom tried to lead moral lives.

The destruction had been random, meaningless, cruel.

Suddenly, Elijah raised his face to the heavens. He looked up at the black, ugly clouds. The rain splattered on his face. Anger rose in him in a terrible, boiling wave. He shook his fist at heaven. "You did this terrible thing! You're a cruel God!" he screamed. The wind tore the words from his lips and scattered them across the town. "You are mocking us! You've crushed my people like insects. You wrecked the church I built for you. All for no reason. No reason. I don't love you any more. You hear me? I despise you! I curse you."

The world around him swam.

The earth tilted.

He sprawled on the ground in a faint.

The rain fell on him.

Chapter Fourteen

Night had fallen. Jeff and Cave Altman had hung lanterns around the wreckage of their general store and settled down to guard their merchandise through the night. Since the storm, they had taken turns standing guard. As Sid Milam had pointed out, with the new sheriff taking ruthless measures there would probably be no more looting. However, the Altman brothers were taking no chances. Much of the store's merchandise had been ruined by the incessant rain pouring through the torn roof. Yet there were many valuable goods still intact.

Jeff was on the first watch. He had nailed canvas over a section near the front of the store and settled under it, keeping a loaded shotgun close by. He sat in a chair under a lantern and looked out at the night. Shapes of wrecked

125

buildings along Main Street looked like hulking blobs in the pitch-back darkness. Here and there a lamp or lantern gave a feeble glow. For a while, the rain would subside into a drizzle, then turn again into a heavy downpour.

Suddenly, a figure came out of the darkness. Jeff Altman became alert, reaching for the shotgun. The figure moved closer, into the faint circle of light from the lantern.

Altman felt a shock. He was looking at Will Mariott. The newspaper man's face was streaked with blood. His clothes, soaked by the rain, were torn.

The merchant jumped to his feet. "Will. What's happened to you?"

Mariott did not reply. He appeared to be in some kind of emotional state that bordered on collapse. He looked as if he were making a superhuman effort to hold himself together.

A few seconds passed, then Mariott said in low voice, "Jeff, do you have any guns for sale?"

"What are you talking about, Will? Listen, sit down, man. You look terrible."

"I asked if you have any guns you can sell."

"Well, yeah, we have some that we were able to keep out of the rain. What do you need a gun for, Will?"

"I need to buy a gun, Jeff. I want a six-gun and some dry shells."

"You look like you're having some bad trouble, Will. Do you want some help? Do you want me to call my brother?"

"I just want to buy the gun. Show me what you have."

Altman took down the lantern and led the way to a protected area covered by canvas. He pulled back the canvas,
revealing an assortment of rifles, shotguns, and pistols.

Mariott selected a Colt .45 and a belt and holster. He
strapped on the gun belt. "Now I'll need the cartridges."

Altman took a box from under a counter. Mariott opened
the revolver and carefully inserted six cartridges in the
empty chambers, then closed the gun. He thrust the gun
into the holster. "How much do I owe you, Jeff?"

Altman told him the price of the gun and ammunition.
Mariott took a handful of gold coins from his pocket. "I'm
sure that's enough," he said.

"Wait a minute, Will. Don't you want me to count it? I
think you've given me too much."

But Will Mariott had already moved out of the circle of
lantern light, fading into the darkness. Jeff Altman stared
after him, puzzled and troubled. He heard Mariott's foot-
steps on the boardwalk fading off. Then there was just the
darkness and the sound of the rain.

Will Mariott walked the length of Main Street to Mexican Joe's saloon on the outskirts of town. It was a long
walk and Mariott was unsteady on his feet.

Mexican Joe's place was the one island of light in the
pitch-black town. There was the sound of voices in the
saloon. Men had come here after a day of building coffins,
digging graves, and cleaning storm debris to numb their
feelings of helplessness and despair with Mexican Joe's
liquor.

Will Mariott entered the place. The sound of voices died

down as the men in the place turned to stare at the rain-soaked figure with the bloody face and glassy eyes standing in the doorway.

Mariott saw what he had come for: Smith's deputy, standing at the end of the bar. He said, "You filthy dog; I'm going to kill you."

The other men along the bar hastily got out of the way. Mariott reached for his revolver. He had it half drawn when the deafening report of a gun slammed across the room.

Will Mariott staggered backward.

Smith, at a table some distance from the bar, holding his smoking revolver, arose from his chair. He fired five more times, emptying the chamber of his pistol. All of the bullets struck Will Mariott, throwing him against a wall, turning his shirtfront to a bloody pulp. His gun tumbled from his hand. He was dead before he slid to the floor.

Chapter Fifteen

At the Houston ranch, Link was not aware of the events taking place in Endless that Monday. He had spent a miserable Sunday night, kept awake by the pain from his leg. The last of the laudanum had been used. He had substituted a bottle of whiskey.

Link stared up at the pitch blackness, listening to the steady patter of rain on the barn roof. A few feet away, Laura was asleep on her cot. He could hear her soft breathing and occasional stirring in her sleep. By filling his mind with her sweet, young image, he could get his mind temporarily off his throbbing leg. He visualized her soft gold hair, blue eyes, smooth, fair skin. He let his imagination roam, smoothing back her hair, tasting her lips, hearing her voice croon pleasure as his kisses roamed down to

129

her throat. The thoughts made his blood pound. His entire being was filled with his love for her and his hunger for her. The sound of her voice, her movements, her innocent, kind nature filled him with tender caring.

Until he met Laura, his thoughts had all revolved around himself. Now he had learned what it meant to love someone so fiercely that he must view his life and his desires in terms of another person.

For the first time, Link experienced a wave of guilt at dragging Laura into his life. What had started out as a flirtation and romantic conquest had turned into a dangerous cloud over Laura's life. He had made her fall in love with him. She was a gentle girl who had led the sheltered life of a preacher's daughter. Now she was involved with a man hiding out from the law. Maybe she thought at this point it was romantic. There was nothing romantic about being constantly on the run from bounty hunters. The Mexican border meant nothing to a bounty hunter intent on bringing Link Houston's dead body back for reward money. Bounty hunters would trail him no matter how deep into Mexico he fled. That's what she would have to live with if Link took her to Mexico with him.

Being awake and in pain at 2:00 A.M. is a lonely experience, when a man has nowhere to hide from himself. At a time like that, his mortality becomes very real. He stands on the frightening brink of an unknown eternity, facing a God he doesn't understand, but fears. He is forced to take stock of his life, uneasy at the weighing of his character, at the list of his sins and shortcomings that are exaggerated, perhaps out of proportion. He searches for some redeeming aspects of his existence and ends by despising himself.

That night became a turning point in Link's life. He was confronted with a fearful decision. The choice could be the difference between life and death for himself. It could also be the difference between life and death for the girl he loved.

Whatever road he chose, his future would never be the same.

As he drank enough to keep the pain numbed, he became increasingly obsessed with the conviction that for Laura's sake as well as his own, he must clear his name of the murder charge.

The more he thought about it, the more convinced he became that he should question the jurors. In addition, there were two other people he wanted to pin down for some answers. One was Walt Sawyer, the town drunk who swore he saw Link leave the bank building the night Albert Milam was shot. If anyone had been bribed, it was most likely Walt Sawyer. And there was the bank teller, Jake Simms. Why had he sworn at the trial that Link threatened to kill Albert Milam? Link had made no such threat. Was Simms trying to cover up his own involvement? Had he been dipping into the bank's funds? Maybe Albert caught him. Maybe Simms committed the murder to protect himself. Then he pinned the shooting on Link by bribing Walt Sawyer and lying about Link's threat to kill the banker.

By the time dawn arrived that Monday morning, Link

had convinced himself that he stood a good chance of clearing his name if he acted fast.

When he told Ben of his decision, his father exploded
with disgust. "Link, you been tilting that bottle all night.
It's the whiskey talking. If you've got any sense at all,
you'll stay hid until your leg is well enough for you to
make the trip to Mexico."

Maybe, Link admitted, he was a little drunk, but his mind
was made up.

Laura didn't have any more success at talking him out
of leaving the safety of the barn. She made a breakfast of
biscuits and coffee over an open fire while Ben and Link
argued.

"Link, sometimes I don't think you've got the sense you
were born with," Ben stormed. "If you go around talking
to the people that was on that jury, they're bound to spread
the word that you've come back here. The talk will get to
that new sheriff and he'll be out here, gunning for you."

Link stood his ground. "If he's the law and I've found
some evidence that clears me, he's got to see that I get a
new trial."

"From what I've heard about that man, he shoots and
then asks questions. Besides, if somebody else killed Albert
Milam, he's not going to sit quietly back while you turn
him in. If the sheriff don't blow your fool brains out, Milam's killer will."

"What did you mean, 'if somebody else killed Albert
Milam?' You still think maybe I did it, don't you?" Link
said angrily.

"I'm trying to believe you, but I know how hotheaded you can be sometimes. Like right now, with this crazy notion you got in your head to talk to them jurors."

"I'm not asking your advice or permission. I just want to know if I can borrow your buckboard."

"Sure," Ben yelled. "You're welcome to it. Go get your darn fool self killed. Sure make my life a lot simpler." Then he stormed out of the barn.

Link fitted the crutches Ben had brought from town under his arms and painfully stood up. By keeping all the weight on his good leg, he was able to hold the broken leg with the cast from touching the ground as he tried some experimental steps.

Laura said in a worried voice, "Link, do you think your father's right, that you're taking too much of a chance, going around where people will see you?"

"I have to do it, Laura. I studied about this real hard, all night. If I don't find the real killer and clear my name, somewhere down the line it's going to catch up with me. Sure, we might get across the border where the law can't reach me. But you can be sure Sid Milam will put a price on my head. He'll want his brother's killer brought to justice. Once there's a reward out, professional bounty hunters will be after me. Men like this new sheriff, Smith, think nothing of crossing the Mexican border to get that bounty money. When the reward says 'dead or alive,' you can be sure it means 'dead' to a bounty hunter. It's a lot simpler to sneak a dead man back across the Rio Grande." Link shook his head. "My best chance is right here, finding the killer while people are too wrapped up with what the storm did to them to bother about catching up with me. I'll need your help, though, Laura. I can't manage the wagon with my leg busted like it is.''

''Of course I'll do whatever you want me to, Link. I just hope it's the right thing.''

They found enough slickers stored in the barn to keep dry. Laura went out and hitched up the buckboard.

Using his crutches, Link painfully hobbled out to the wagon and struggled up on the seat beside Laura.

''Now what?'' she asked.

''Walt Sawyer and Jake Simms. They were the state's two strongest witnesses against me. Without them, the state wouldn't have had a case. Walt lives in a shack near the edge of town. I reckon we can take a chance on seeing him. But Jake Simms would be down at Sid Milam's bank, helping get the place cleaned up. It would be too risky for me to be seen on Main Street.''

''All right, let's go talk to Walt.''

They found Walt Sawyer living in a tent in his yard. There was nothing left of the shack that had been his home except a pile of scattered boards. Sawyer was sprawled on a cot in the tent, dead drunk.

Link stood just inside the tent, supporting himself with his crutches. Disgustedly, he said, ''Well, we sure won't get anything out of him in that condition.''

''What can we do?''

''Sober him up somehow.''

Link looked at the empty bottles strewn around the cot.

"It's going to take some doing. Looks like he's been drunk ever since the tornado hit on Friday. Laura, honey, I saw a barrel full of rainwater in the yard. There's a bucket in the wagon. Please fill it with water and bring it in here. Dousing him with cold rainwater should go a long way to sobering him up."

Laura nodded. She added, wrinkling her nose, "It'll give him a bath at the same time, which he surely needs."

When Laura carried the filled bucket into the tent, Link retrieved the bottle of whiskey from beside Walt, then nodded toward the cot. Laura poured the entire contents of the bucket on the snoring drunk.

Walt sat up, spluttering and cursing. He was drenched to the skin. He glanced around with a befuddled expression. He looked so comical, Laura giggled.

He began shivering. "Wha's goin' on? I need a drink."

When Sawyer saw the bottle Link was holding, he cried, "Gimme some of that," and made a grab for the bottle.

Link kept it out of his reach. "You don't get any of this until you answer some questions, Walt."

For the first time, Sawyer appeared to realize who he was talking to. "Link Houston," he gasped. "I thought they sent you off to Huntsville."

"Well, they nearly did, but the tornado hit the stagecoach and I got away."

"Oh, that tornado was the most god-awful thing ever happened to me," Sawyer said in a quavering voice. "Blew my house plumb away. Scared me so bad I still ain't got over it." Tears were trickling down his cheeks. "I need a drink real bad. See how my hand is shaking?"

"I'll give you something to drink in a minute. First, I want you to answer some questions."

Then Sawyer noticed Laura. He squinted his eyes, bringing her into focus. "Why, you're Miss Laura Sontag, the preacher's daughter."

"Yes, I am."

"What're you doin' here? Where are we, anyway? I'm all wet. How'd I get so wet?"

"You're in your tent. You're wet because we poured a bucket of water over you."

"Why'd you go and do that?" he whined.

"To sober you up enough to talk to me. I want to know why you lied about me at the trial."

Sawyer looked frightened. "I don't know what you're talking about. Listen, I need a drink real bad."

"You lied, Walt. You told that jury that you saw me coming out of the bank building the night Albert Milam was murdered. That's a rotten lie. Who paid you to say that, Walt?"

The small man was beginning to shake. "I tell you, I need a drink," he whined. "I'm wet and cold. I'm gettin' a chill."

"You ain't getting a swallow until you tell me what I want to know. Whoever killed Albert Milam paid you to lie at the trial. I want to know who it was."

Sawyer's face had turned ashen. He became engaged in a life-and-death struggle between fear and his craving for alcohol. "I thought I seen you coming out of the bank that night, Link," he said, his teeth chattering. "Maybe I was wrong, but I swear I thought it was you."

"No you didn't. By that time of night you would have been too drunk to recognize anybody. You got paid to lie. Was it Jake Simms, the bank teller? He lied, too. He would have reason to shoot Albert Milam if he was stealing from the bank and got caught."

"I don't know nothing about that. Can't you see I'm a sick man?" he whined. "Please, just one drink."

The argument went on for a while with Walt Sawyer becoming increasingly agitated and demoralized. Finally, his craving for alcohol overcame his fear. "All right," he said in a frightened voice. "I'll tell you the truth, but you got to swear you won't tell nobody what I'm going to say." He looked pleadingly at Link. "I've been told that I'll get shot if I talk about this to anyone."

"We're just trying to get at the truth," Link said. "We're not going to talk to anyone about what you say."

Sawyer was shaking badly. "First, I got to have that drink."

Link poured a small amount in a tin cup. "That's just for starters. Tell us what you know and I'll give you the bottle."

Sawyer took the cup. Holding it in both hands, he swallowed the contents in a gulp. He wiped the back of his hand across his mouth. He looked around fearfully, then spoke in a low, frightened voice. "Jake Simms, the teller at the bank, came to me the morning after the banker was shot. He gave me some money to go tell the sheriff I'd seen you sneaking away from the bank right after Albert Milam was shot. Later, he promised me some more money if I'd testify at the trial. Now, gimme the bottle. You promised.''

They left Sawyer sitting on his cot, shivering and gulping liquor from his bottle. On the wagon, Laura picked up the reins.

''Jake Simms!'' Link exclaimed. ''Didn't I tell you, Laura? Jake Simms! I've suspected all along that he did it.''

''Do you reckon Mr. Sawyer was telling you the truth? Bad as he wanted that bottle of whisky, he'd say just about anything.''

''You're right, of course. This is a start,'' Link said, ''but I'm going to need a lot more. The other thing is the jury. I still need to find out if some of the jurors were bribed, and why. That part doesn't add up. If Jake Simms killed Albert Milam, it makes good sense that he'd pay Walt Sawyer to lie about seeing me around the bank that night. It doesn't make sense that Simms would turn around at the same time and bribe some men on the jury to try and get me off, unless his conscience got to bothering him, and I doubt that. Let's go talk to the jury foreman, Caster Lambert.''

Lambert was a poor sharecropper on a small piece of land owned by Sid Milam. His farm was several miles from town. Getting there meant a rough ride over narrow, caliche-topped lanes and through gravel-bed arroyos. The arroyos had filled with rainwater several feet deep. The horse slogged through the water that swirled around the buckboard up to the hubs of the wheels. The rain poured down steadily, relentlessly.

The rough ride on the wagon sent jolts of pain though Link. He took several drinks from his whiskey bottle to ease the pain.

The drinking upset Laura. She said, "I heard my daddy preach against the evils of drink so often, it pains me to see you using hard liquor, Link."

"It's just to ease the pain, Laura. When my leg stops hurting, I won't touch another drop."

"Thank you. That would make me happy. It would make me happy if you and your daddy got along better, too."

"He's a stubborn old coot with an ornery streak," Link said. "A lot of things in his life have made him bitter. The war, losing his arm, my mother running off with another man. Ben ain't had an easy life. And I didn't help any with my wild ways. I guess once you lose trust in somebody, the way he has for me, it's mighty hard to get it back. But I'm going to lead a different life, Laura, for your sake. I promise."

She squeezed his hand. "I believe you, Link. I love you and I trust you."

"That's what's keepin' me going now, Laura, honey."

At last they arrived at the gate to Lambert's farm. The gate had been blown down by the storm as had most of the fence. The small farmhouse and barn had been severely damaged.

Caster Lambert, a slender man in baggy overalls covered with a slicker, was stacking pieces of wet lumber beside the ruined house in the rain. He looked up at the sound of the wagon entering his yard. Some dogs came from the back of the yard and ran up to the wagon, barking furiously. Lambert called them off.

The farmer went up to meet the wagon. He peered near-sightedly through steel-rimmed glasses at the wagon's occupants. When he recognized Link, his eyes widened and his jaw dropped. For a moment he was speechless. Then he gasped, "Link Houston! Are you a ghost? I heard the tornado hit the stagecoach and killed everyone on it."

"Guess I was lucky, Caster. I got off with a broke leg."

The farmer nodded to Laura, touching the brim of his hat. "Mornin', Miss Laura. I'm about as surprised to see you as I am to see Link. How is your daddy?"

"All right, I reckon," she replied, "though he's about out of his mind with grief over all the people hurt and killed by the storm."

Caster nodded sadly. "It's a terrible thing. I lost about everything I owned," he said, waving his hand in a hope-less gesture at the ruined house and barn. For a moment his shoulders slumped and a look of utter defeat crossed his weather-beaten face. Then he pulled himself together and said, "I've fixed up a little shelter over by the barn. Come on out of the rain. I swear, it looks like it ain't never going to stop."

He helped Link down from the wagon seat. They went a short distance to a makeshift shed the farmer had put together, and sat on boxes out of the rain.

"I know you're trying to figure out what we're doing here, Mr. Lambert," Link said. "I've come to ask your help. I know you're a decent, honest man, and you wouldn't want to see a man hung for something he didn't do. The tornado that hit Endless was a terrible thing, but it has given me a chance to clear my name. The fact is, no matter what you heard in court, I didn't kill Albert Milam. I was miles away in a card game that night, just like I swore in court.

"Somebody else killed that banker and tried to make it look like I done it, and I think I've found out who it was. We talked to Walt Sawyer this morning. He admitted that the bank teller, Jake Simms, paid him to lie about seeing me at the bank building that night Milam was shot. The way I figure it, Albert Milam found out that Simms was stealing money from the bank so Simms killed him. That part is clear enough. But there's something else that doesn't fit in. Just before he died, the lawyer, Crenshaw, told my Dad that he thought some jurors had been bribed to keep me from getting hung. If Jake Simms paid Walt Sawyer to pin the murder on me, why would he turn around and bribe the jury to let me off with a lighter sentence? You were the foreman on that jury. What do you make of all this?"

Caster Lambert was silent for several minutes. There was no sound except the steady patter of rain. Then the farmer said, "Well, you're partly right in what you found out,

Link. But you're partly wrong, too. Jake Simms did bribe Walt Sawyer to lie about you. But there's a whole lot more to this whole situation than you can imagine. It involves some very powerful people.

"I'll tell you truthfully, I was one on the jury that was given money to try and get you off. I wouldn't have taken it except I wasn't entirely convinced you'd shot Albert Milam. I know it was dishonest of me to take that money, but times have been awfully hard for folks like me. I haven't been able to raise a crop in two years because of the drought. I had to shoot my cows because they were starving to death. I was close to starving myself."

He stood up. "I think the time has come that you can find out what is behind all of this—the killing, the false testimony, the lies, the bribes. I'm going to take you to somebody who can tell you everything."

Chapter Sixteen

Caster Lambert refused to tell them anything else. He said they'd just have to come with him. He saddled a horse and rode beside the wagon as they left his farmyard. He led them to the main road to Endless.

After a few miles, they stopped. Link was totally baffled to see they were at the entrance to Sid Milam's big ranch.

"You two wait here," Lambert said. "I'm pretty sure Mr. Milam is in town, but I want to ride up to the big house and make certain."

After a while, Lambert returned and motioned for them to follow him up to the main house.

"I've heard of this place," Laura said with a touch of awe in her voice. "It must be the biggest, finest house in the whole world."

"At least this side of San Antonio or Monterey," Link agreed.

"Why do you reckon Mr. Lambert has brought us here?"

"I don't know," Link said, beginning to feel nervous. Why, indeed, would Caster Lambert bring them to the home of the man whose brother Link was accused of murdering?

"Maybe it's some kind of trap," Laura said anxiously. She hugged Link's arm. "Maybe we ought to get out of here."

Lambert dismounted and came to the wagon to help Link get down. "Don't be afraid," he said. "Mr. Milam and all of his hands are in town cleaning up the bank building. Mrs. Milam and her maid are the only ones here."

Link decided to trust the farmer. He struggled out of the wagon seat and fitted his crutches under his arms. Lambert helped him up the steps, across the wide veranda, and through the front entrance. They were in a long hallway paved with gleaming tile. Above them were giant beams. The walls of the sprawling ranch house were adobe brick, two feet thick, to keep out the heat in summer and the cold in winter.

A woman servant appeared and took their wet rain slickers. She provided them with towels to help dry off and laid a piece of carpet on the floor to wipe the mud from their feet.

From the hallway they went into the main room. Like the hallway, the floor was shiny Mexican tile, but covered in places with thick area rugs. The furniture was heavy, dark mahogany, hand-carved in Mexico. On one side of the room was an enormous fireplace. Above it was mounted the horns of a longhorn steer measuring a good eight feet from tip to tip. On the walls were paintings, Indian blankets, and deer horns.

Laura stared wide-eyed at the opulence that surrounded her.

Seated on the couch was Angelita Milam. She arose and crossed the room to meet them.

Laura had seen Sid Milam's wife a few times in town in a carriage, but always at a distance. Now, seeing her up close, Laura found her beauty breathtaking. She had the classic features and delicate complexion of a pure, aristocratic Spanish heritage. Her large, dark eyes were luminous. Her black hair was gathered at the nape of her neck in a bun. She wore a costly diamond-studded necklace and bracelet. There were heavy gold rings and diamonds on the fingers of the hand she extended in greeting.

She was very poised and gracious, but her eyes revealed inner emotional turmoil. In flawless English she said fervently, "I'm so happy to see you alive, Mr. Houston. We all thought you had been killed by the tornado."

"I guess you could call it a miracle, Mrs. Milam. Far as I could tell, everyone else on the stagecoach was killed."

"Mr. Lambert told me about your injured leg. I'm so sorry, but at least, thank God, you're alive. Please, sit right here." She indicated a large, comfortable chair.

She got her emotions under control and turned to Laura.

"You are the daughter of Reverend Sontag. You are such a beautiful young woman. If I had a daughter, I would wish her to look like you."

Then she touched Laura's golden hair. "Forgive me. It is a Mexican custom to touch something we admire so it will not bring bad luck to the other person."

"Thank you, Ma'am," Laura said. She had never met a woman with such a gracious, noble air. She felt as if she were in the presence of royalty.

"Now, please be seated. Let me offer you something to drink. A glass of sherry, perhaps?"

"Thank you," Laura stammered, "I do not drink alcoholic beverages."

"Of course. Your church forbids it. I respect and admire you for having convictions. A glass of fruit juice, then?"

Laura nodded. "Yes, ma'am. That would be fine."

"And you, Mr. Houston?"

"Well, ma'am, my religion doesn't stand between me and alcohol and right now with my leg hurting, I'd be most obliged for a drink of bourbon and branch water."

"You shall certainly have it. And the same for you, Mr. Lambert?"

"Yes, ma'am. That would be fine." Lambert took a seat in a nearby chair.

Angelita Milam clapped her hands. The servant appeared. Angelita spoke in rapid Spanish. The maid left, then returned shortly with a tray of drinks which she passed around.

Laura tasted her drink. It was delicious, sweet orange

juice, freshly squeezed. "It's from oranges on our trees,"
Angelita said. Then she turned her attention to Link. She
drew a straight-back chair with a rawhide seat closer and
took a seat, facing him.

Some of her carefully controlled poise faltered. She
twisted a ring on her finger nervously. "You have been
through a terrible experience, Mr. Houston, accused of a
crime you did not commit, then being nearly killed in that
horrible storm." Tears filled her eyes. "I am going to beg
your forgiveness because I am partly to blame for what you
have been through. I was so happy when Mr. Lambert told
me you had come back alive. I have much to tell you.
Please try not to judge me too harshly. I want to make
amends, and I think I can help you."

Link stared at her, totally baffled by what she was saying.
How could she possibly be involved in the murder of Albert
Milam? Was this what Caster Lambert meant when he said
the murder of Albert Milam involved some powerful people?

"Were you the person who bribed some of the jurors to
try and get me off?" he exclaimed.

She nodded gravely. "Let me go back ten years, so
you'll understand everything. Ten years ago, Sid Milam
asked for my hand in marriage. It was my father's wish
that I accept the proposal. I was raised to obey my father
in all things, so I agreed to the marriage although I did not
love Sid Milam. Perhaps I could have grown to love him.
That often happens in the arranged marriages that are part
of the Spanish custom. Unfortunately, that was not possible

with Sid Milam. He is a despicable man, cruel, selfish, ruthless. In the place of loving him, I grew to hate and fear him. Because of his anger at my coldness, he often beat me. I only thank God that my father did not live to see how unhappy I have been.

"As you know, the man who was president of my husband's bank, Mack Linden, died suddenly of a heart attack. My husband had his younger brother, Albert Milam, take over operation of the bank. Albert was charming, handsome, attentive, and I've known for a long time that he desired me. A woman senses such things."

A soft pink blush spread over her cheeks and she lowered her eyes. "I was lonely and vulnerable. Although I had grown to hate Sid Milam, I had never been unfaithful. I am ashamed to have to tell you that Albert became my sweetheart. My husband discovered the affair. He was insane with jealousy. He went to the bank that night. He and Albert had a terrible quarrel. My husband shot and killed his brother."

There was a moment of frozen silence in the room. Laura gasped softly. Link stared at Angelita Milam, dumbfounded, his thought processes temporarily frozen. Then he exclaimed, "But the bank teller, Jake Simms, bribed Walt Sawyer to say he'd seen me leave the bank that night. And Simms lied at the trial, saying I'd threatened to kill Albert Milam."

Angelita said, "Jake Simms did all that because he was ordered to do those things. My husband told him to bribe Walt Sawyer. He was ordered to lie at the trial. Mr. Simms has a large family. He needs to keep his job. But more than that, he is afraid of my husband. He was afraid that he, too, would get shot if he didn't do what he was told to do. Sid Milam is a ruthless, dangerous man, Mr. Houston. His only god is power. He owns the town of Endless. He thinks nothing of having anyone killed who crosses him.''

Link suddenly felt an overpowering wave of anger. ''If you knew all that, why didn't you speak up? Why did you put me through all that misery . . . get me a prison sentence?''

Tears trickled from Angelita's large, luminous eyes. ''For the same reason Jake Simms lied. I am a coward. I am afraid of Sid Milam. I knew he would kill me. And what good would it do? I had no proof. The night of the murder, my husband came home. He told me he had killed my lover, and then he beat me unmercifully. It would be my word against the powerful Sid Milam. Who, in this day and time, will listen to a mere woman? A wife can't even testify against her husband in the courts. But I wouldn't have lived to testify, anyway. My life was hanging by a thread after my husband found out about my affair. He came very close to killing me as well as my lover when he found out about the affair.''

She sighed. ''Mr. Houston, I went through hell when I discovered they were going to pin the murder on you. The only thing I could do was try to keep them from hanging you. Sid Milam has gotten control of all the property that belonged to my father. But he let me keep my jewelry. I have quite a fortune in gold and diamond pieces that have been in my family for generations. I went to San Antonio and had some of my jewelry converted to cash. I used that to pay some members of the jury to find you innocent. Mr. Caster Lambert, here, acted as my agent with the jury. He knew which people on the jury could be bribed. He passed my money on to them. They were supposed to convince the rest of the jury to bring in a verdict of not guilty. I'm sorry to say they didn't succeed. There were too many on the jury who were afraid to let you go free. The feeling in the town was running high. There was talk of a lynching. You were known as a young drifter, gambler, and trouble-maker. The town had already tried and convicted you of killing a prominent citizen, the brother of Sid Milam, no less. But the people I'd bribed at least were able to save you from hanging by stubbornly insisted on the lesser charge. The others finally gave in, knowing it would be a hung jury if they didn't, so you got off with a jail sentence. Now you are alive and free. I think Heaven took a hand in this—and has given me a chance to make amends and help you.''

"How can you do that?'' Link asked bitterly. "You think the law would believe me any more now than before?''

"This time, there is another, very important witness. Jake Simms has spoken to me secretly. He has been tortured by his conscience the way I have been. He just can't live knowing he'd put an innocent man behind bars for the rest of his life. He's told me he's ready to put his life on the line—to come forth and testify that my husband ordered him to bribe Walt Sawyer and to lie at the trial. We were going to try and get you a new trial based on that. Then the tornado struck. Now my husband has gotten the mayor to hire some kind of terrible gunman named Smith to act as sheriff. Nobody seems to know where Smith came from or anything about him, but everyone is afraid of him.''

Link nodded. ''I've heard about him.''

''The man is evil personified. If people in town find out you lived through the tornado and are in this area, my husband will have Smith find you and kill you. You must hide until the town gets rid of this evil man. When Endless has recovered from the storm and the right kind of law and order is restored, we'll see about getting you a new trial and clearing your name. Meanwhile, however, you must stay hidden. I have wealthy relatives in Mexico who can protect you. Can you make a trip like that?''

''I guess I could get there in a wagon. I can't ride a horse with my leg in this shape.''

''Then you must plan to make the trip by wagon. Right now, the roads are too muddy for a wagon. You must find a place to hide until the rain stops and the roads are better. Then I'll give you maps and letters to my relatives in Mexico. Also, I'll see that you have money.''

''Thanks, but if I do go to Mexico, Laura is coming with me,'' Link said.

Angelita smiled. ''Young people in love. In spite of the trouble you are in, I envy you.''

When the meeting ended and they rode back to the Houston ranch, Link told his father what had transpired since they left that morning. Ben Houston was dumbfounded. "Sid Milam killed his own brother? I'll be hanged."

"Now maybe you'll be convinced I had nothing to do with Albert Milam's murder," Link said angrily.

Ben didn't reply. Instead, he said, "Link, you're going to have to find someplace else for a hideout until you can leave for Mexico. The folks in town are bound to find out the tornado didn't kill you and you're here with me. If you talked to Walt Sawyer, he'll spread it around. I strongly suspect that new sheriff, Smith, is going to be out here very soon, looking for you. I rode into town while you were gone. Juan Cardoza's body is hanging from a rope tied to the porch of the opera building. Smith lynched him this morning. Claimed he was looting."

"Oh, no!" Laura gasped, her eyes filling with tears. "Juan and his family came to our church. He was a good, simpleminded man. I can't believe he'd steal."

"He was just trying to get some food for his family," Ben said. "The hurricane blew away everything they owned."

"Good Lord, what kind of a monster is this new sheriff?" Link asked.

"A mean one," Ben said angrily. "A real mean one. If Smith finds you here, you'll find yourself hanging from the opera house porch beams alongside Juan Cardoza. And he'll probably shoot me for harboring a fugitive. We need to find you a new hideout until the roads to Mexico dry out enough so a wagon can travel on them. I've got a tent stored here in the barn. I used to spend the night away from the house sometimes when I was out working on fences. There's some high ground on my land some distance from here. You know the place, Link. I'll help you get a camp set up there. It's not likely Smith will find you there.''

Ben and Laura loaded camping supplies in the wagon while Link rested on a cot in the barn.

It was near sundown when they were ready to leave. Ben said, ''The ground is too muddy for us to cross open rangeland. The wagon would bog down before we went a hundred yards. But Link, you remember, there's a creek with a gravel bottom that will take us there. Normally, it's a dry creekbed. Now, because of all the rain, it has water, but it's shallow. An advantage of going up the creekbed is that we won't leave any tracks if they come here looking for you.''

When they reached the campsite, Ben and Laura set up the tent. ''I'll check on you in a couple of days,'' Ben said. ''You have enough food to last that long.''

He left the wagon, two horses, and a saddle with them and rode away, back down the creekbed.

That night, Laura moved her cot beside Link. They held hands as the rain drummed steadily on the canvas above them.

Laura said, ''Listen to that rain. Isn't it ever going to quit?''

''Doesn't look like it. And we're stuck here until the roads get dry.''

Laura sighed. ''The tornado was on Friday. This is Monday night. Just a little over three days, but it's like a whole lifetime. So much has happened to all of us. I don't hardly feel like the same person any more. I feel a lot older. Can you get older in three days?''

''I reckon you can, Laura, honey. I don't feel like the same person, either. But loving you has a lot to do with that.''

''I love you, too, Link. So much. As terrible as the storm has been, at least it brought you back to me.''

''The first thing we'll do when we get to Mexico is get married,'' Link said.

She squeezed his hand in the darkness. ''That will be a happy day for me, Link. I didn't know what it was like to be in love with a man before I met you, but I do now.''

''You're an angel,'' Link said. ''A sweet, innocent angel. I'm going to take good care of you and do everything I can to make you happy. We'll have a place of our own one day, and we'll have a family. Do you want to have kids with me, Laura?''

''Of course I do, when you're my husband. I love children. I know something about raising them because I've been like a mother to my brother and sister.''

Link stared up at the darkness, feeling the warmth of Laura's hand in his. ''I love you so much.''

Laura felt a warm flush all over her body and a powerful yearning deep inside—the most powerful yearning she'd ever experienced. It made her heart beat faster, but it was so overpowering, it frightened her. The emotions raging in her made her shake all over. She touched his lips with her fingers. ''I don't know much about being married,'' she whispered. "I didn't have a mother to tell me about it. I do want to make you happy, Link," she whispered.

"I want to do the same for you. I guess that's a big part of being in love, my sweetheart."

She squeezed his hand. "Link, I just have to visit my brother and sister one more time before we go to Mexico. I have to tell them goodbye. And I have to see my father and make sure he's all right."

Link frowned, trying to see her face in the darkness. "When do you plan to do that?"

"I can go early in the morning. I'll be back before dark. It tears me up to leave you alone here, but I don't know when I'll ever see my family again. I love them, too, you know. Not the way I love you, but I do love them. We may have to spend the rest of our lives in Mexico and I'd never see them again. I just have to tell them goodbye."

"I understand," Link said. "I'll be all right here. But I'm worried about you riding into town alone."

"There's nothing to worry about. It's not me they're looking for."

They fell silent. Link, exhausted from the pain in his leg, went to sleep, holding Laura's hand. She couldn't sleep. The darkness was complete and intense. Not a single star penetrated the heavy clouds. She saw only blackness, and she was afraid. Some kind of evil force had descended on Endless and spread through all their lives. Going to Mexico with Link was a beautiful dream, but in her heart she didn't believe the dream would come true. The evil force was not through with them. Something unspeakably terrible was going to happen to them very soon . . .

Chapter Seventeen

The next morning, Tuesday, Sheriff Smith rode down Main Street to the site of Sid Milam's bank, where workers were laboring to clean up the debris. He dismounted and strode to the tent where Sid Milam had set up a temporary office.

When Smith entered the tent, Milam arose from behind a makeshift desk to greet him.

"I got word you wanted to see me," Smith said.

"Yes. I have a problem I'd like for you to handle."

Milam paced around the small area restlessly, rubbing the back of his neck as he arranged his thoughts. He had more than one problem. Last night, in a gunfight at Mexican Joe's saloon, Smith had shot and killed Will Mariott. There was no question about it being a matter of self-defense. The newspaper man had drawn his gun first. Milam wondered angrily what in heaven's name had gotten into Will Mariott. He was a newspaper man, not a gunslinger. He had burst into Mexican Joe's saloon in an agitated state and drawn his gun on one of Smith's deputies. Smith had no choice but to shoot.

Mariott was well liked and highly regarded in the town. Coming so soon after the lynching of Juan Cardoza, his death had the citizens of Endless in a state of nervous rebellion over this new sheriff. They were blaming Sid Milam for giving him the job.

Well, Milam thought, he could handle them. It was too bad about Cardoza and Will Mariott, but in a little over two days, since he rode into town late Saturday, Smith had put a stop to the looting and gotten the town under control. There might be some grumbling about his strong-arm methods, but he was getting the job done.

At the moment, what had Sid Milam more disturbed was some information that had come to him this morning. It was something that affected him personally.

He explained the matter to Smith: "Recently, my younger brother, Albert, who had the job of president of my bank, was murdered in cold blood by a young renegade from this area, Link Houston. This Houston fellow is the son of a local rancher, Ben Houston. Ben had his hands full raising Link. The boy was always in trouble—gambling debts, fights. Ben finally ran him off. Link came back a few months ago. He's been hanging around the area, gambling and drinking. He got in a fight with my brother over

a loan Ben Houston owes the bank. That night, he went up
to Albert's office at the bank and shot him. A jury found
him guilty of Albert's murder, but he got off with a jail
sentence. Why they didn't do the job right and hang him
is something nobody can figure out. Anyway, Sheriff Matt
Blake put him on the stage Friday with one of his deputies,
taking him to Huntsville. A few miles out of town, the stage
got hit by the tornado. Blew it all to pieces. We figured
everybody on the stage was killed. Turns out maybe Link
Houston wasn't killed. He's had the gall to come back here
to Endless. I want him found and brought to justice for
killing my brother. I'm putting up a reward of five hundred
dollars, dead or alive.''

Smith listened, his face showing no emotion. "How did
you find out he'd come back here?"

"Walt Sawyer told several people he saw Link yesterday
morning. Claims he talked with him."

"Who is this Walt Sawyer?"

"Oh, he's something of the town drunk. Lives in a shack
at the west end of town."

"If he's the town drunk, how do you know he's telling
the truth?"

"Maybe he isn't. I don't know why he'd make up a story
like that, though. I wish you'd check it out."

Smith nodded, his eyes cold and hard. "For a five-
hundred-dollar reward, you can bet I'll check it out, and if
this Houston fellow is around, I'll bring him in."

Milam watched Smith leave the tent, ducking under the
flaps. He shivered. The man gave him cold chills. He

wouldn't want to be in the shoes of any man Smith was after. But he felt a sense of relief. If it was true Link Houston had come back, Smith would certainly find him and deal with him.

Smith rode to Walt Sawyer's place. He found Sawyer in a tent near the remains of his shack. He was sitting on the edge of his cot holding his head, nursing a hangover. The place smelled of sour whiskey.

Smith gave him a disgusted look. "Your name Walt Sawyer?"

Walt looked up. When he recognized the tall man silhouetted in the entrance to his tent, he felt a chill of apprehension. Everyone in town was afraid of this man.

"Yessir," he replied.

"Stand up."

Sawyer got shakily to his feet. The room tilted. He swayed, trying to keep upright.

"You sober enough to understand me?"

"Yessir."

"You're telling it around town that you saw Link Houston yesterday. Is that truth?"

"Yessir, it is. He was standing right there where you are now. Miss Laura Sontag was with him."

"Who is Laura Sontag?"

"She's the preacher's daughter."

"What was she doing here?"

"Well, she come here with Link. There was some talk before he was arrested for murder that she was sweet on him. I reckon she still is. When they left, I saw them ride off in a wagon. Miss Laura was driving the wagon. Link's got a busted leg. He was on crutches. I guess he can't handle the wagon very well with his leg like that.''

"Why did he come here to talk to you?''

"Well, you see, at the trial I testified that I seen Link leaving the bank building that night right after he shot Albert Milam. Link come here tryin' to make me say I just made that up.''

"Did you?''

Walt swallowed hard. He wiped the back of his hand across his mouth. His eyes shifted nervously. "No sir . . . I wouldn't tell a lie in a courtroom where I was under oath.''

Walt felt Smith's jet-black-eyed gaze go right through him. He suddenly needed a drink desperately.

The sheriff took two strides into the tent and grabbed a fistful of Walt's shirt in his gloved fist. He gave Sawyer a hard shaking. "You better be telling me the truth now, you miserable little weasel.''

"I am," Walt blubbered. "I swear to God.''

"Did Link Houston say where he was hiding out?''

"No sir," Sawyer whimpered. "But I reckon he's been at his daddy's place.''

"The rancher, Ben Houston?''

"Yessir.''

"You think he's been there since the storm hit the stage-coach?''

"I don't know where else he'd go.''

"Where can I find Houston's girlfriend?''

"Her daddy, the preacher, has been staying in a shelter over on the lot where they were building the new church. Maybe he'd know where she is."

"I'm going to check all this out. If I find out you've been lying to me, you'd better wish you'd died in the tornado."

Smith turned and strode out of the tent. Walt's legs gave way. He collapsed on the cot. He grabbed a bottle. His hand was shaking so hard, the neck of the bottle rattled against his teeth.

Chapter Eighteen

Earlier that morning, Laura had saddled the extra horse Ben had given them and started down the creek to the main road. She expected to be back by nightfall.

Link was left with the buckboard and a horse. He would have a hard time hitching the other horse by himself, but if for some reason he had to get away from here, he could probably manage.

She had kissed Link and clung to him, torn between not wanting to leave him even for a few hours and wanting to tell her family goodbye. Finally, she had pulled herself from his arms and ridden away.

At the home of Anne Wallace, Laura's brother and sister greeted her with shouts of joy, running to leap into her arms. She was delighted to see them clean, well fed, and

162

cared for. She thanked Anne Wallace and promised that their father would take the children off her hands as soon as he had some kind of house for them to live in.

"Don't you fret yourself about them at all, Laura," Anne Wallace said. "They're welcome to stay here as long as they need to. I know what you folks have been through, losing your home and everything. Keeping the children is the least I can do. Now, I want you to change into some clean, dry clothes. I've got another pair of my husband's Levi's and a shirt you can wear. They won't fit any better than the ones you're wearing now, but at least they're clean and dry."

Paul and Ruth were puzzled when Laura hugged them and told them she might have to be gone for a while. "Why can't you stay here with us?" Paul asked tearfully. "We missed you."

"I know, honey. It won't be for long."

That was a lie, she knew. It was possible she would never see them again. She hurried away before they saw the tears in her eyes.

From the Wallace home, Laura rode into Endless. She got there shortly before noon. Not much had changed since Sunday. The rain was still falling in a steady drizzle on the wrecked buildings and piles of debris. The only change she saw were numerous tents and tarps rigged up for protection against the rain.

She found her father under the shelter in the churchyard. She was relieved that he now appeared in full possession of his faculties, but she was shocked at how old and tired he looked. She thought he had aged ten years since she had seen him on Sunday.

When she tied the reins of the horse and ducked into the shelter, Elijah rose and put his arms around her. "Where have you been, Laura? Where are Paul and Ruth?"

"They're just fine, Pa. They're staying with Mrs. Wallace. I was staying with friends."

"I must have lost my senses for several days. My memory is all jumbled up. They tell me the tornado hit Friday afternoon. This is Tuesday morning. I can't remember exactly what I've been doing. It's all mixed up in my head. This is the first day my mind has been clear."

"You got hit on the back of the head by a flying board, Pa."

Elijah shook his head sadly. "It was more than physical hurt, Laura. It's a hurt I feel down in my soul." Elijah took a seat on a log under the tarp. "Here, sit down beside me, Laura, honey." He clasped her hand. "It's been the shock and grief. You just don't know the sights I've seen. Things that tear the heart right out of a man. Nettie Dickerson, holding her dead baby in her arms. We can't get her to give up the child's body so it can be buried. She just sits there, hugging him and crooning to him. Billy Younger, both legs smashed so bad they had to be amputated. He's only sixteen years old. Old people without homes anymore. People who have lost everything. People without hope. And poor old Juan Cardoza, hung by that new sheriff."

Elijah shook his head. "I don't understand the evil that has come to this town. How could God let this happen to us? I've been reading the Bible, studying the story of Job real hard, trying to find some understanding. Job had all kinds of terrible things happen to him, but he never lost his faith. I can't find any comfort in the story. I don't understand how God lets bad things like this happen to good, decent people. Maybe if I'd had better schooling, if I could have gone to one of those religious seminaries, they could have explained it in a way I could understand. But I just learned religion from listening to my daddy preach, and from studying the Bible. Maybe it wasn't enough. Laura, I've lost my faith. I can't preach any more. My heart ain't in it now. I don't believe God cares about us or He wouldn't have brought these terrible afflictions on us.''

"Oh, Pa," Laura said, "preaching is your whole life. I can't think of you in any way but being a preacher. What will you do?"

"Right now, I don't know. Maybe construction work. I'm handy with tools. There's going to be plenty of work for carpenters, rebuilding this town.''

"But I feel so bad about you losing faith. I'll admit mine's been tested real bad, but I haven't lost it altogether. I'll pray for you real hard.''

He patted her hand. "You go ahead and do that, though I don't think it will do any good.''

They were silent for several minutes. Laura's heart was heavy. Her father had been the anchor in her life, the rock that was never moved. Now that was swept away.

"Pa," she said, "I have something to tell you. I'm sorry to put this burden on you with all the other things on your mind, but you have to know. Link Houston has come back. He was hurt when the tornado hit the stagecoach. His leg was broken, but he wasn't killed. I've been with him since the storm. Link never killed Albert Milam, Pa. We've found out who did.''

She related yesterday's events—the surprising revelation of Angelita Milam. "We have to go to Mexico for a while, Pa. Mrs. Milam has relatives there who will take care of us. When things get back to normal here, Link will get a new trial and clear his name.''

Elijah listened solemnly. "Do you truly love the boy, Laura?''

"I truly do, Pa. With all my heart.''

"Then I reckon you should be with him. I was very much against the boy, especially when he was charged with that murder. Now it looks like we done him an injustice. I keep thinking of you as a little girl, but your Ma was your age when I married her. You're old enough to know when things are right between you and a man. I'm sorry that you've picked a course that's going to be so hard, having to hide in Mexico and all, but if you're sure in your heart that it's the thing for you to do . . . It's what you'll do anyway, no matter what I say. Just remember all the time that I'm your daddy and I love you.''

"And I love you, Daddy,'' she said, resting her head on his shoulder. He held her for a while, his strong arm around her. She closed her eyes for a few minutes, pretending she was a little girl again, safe and secure beside him. Then the feeling passed, leaving her a little frightened at the adulthood that had come to her life so suddenly.

She arose. "I need to get back to Link, Pa."

He stood up. They started to leave the shelter of the canvas.

A rider came into the yard, the hooves of his horse splashing through the mud puddles. He dismounted and approached them. He was a very tall man with piercing black eyes. When his rain slicker flapped open, Laura saw two revolvers on his gun belt and a sheriff's badge pinned to his shirt pocket. He said, "Are you Miss Laura Sontag?"

Suddenly, Laura felt very cold. This was the new sheriff she'd heard about, then man who had lynched poor old Juan Cardoza.

"Yes," she said in a low voice.

"Then you need to come with me."

"Why?"

"Because you're under arrest."

"Just a minute," Elijah said angrily, stepping between them. "My daughter ain't done nothing wrong. What do you mean, she's under arrest?"

"She's under arrest for aiding and abetting a fugitive from justice—one Link Houston."

"What kind of proof do you have?" Elijah demanded. "You have to have a legal paper—a warrant."

"I don't have to have anything. Now, either you come with me peacefully, Miss Sontag, or I'll add resisting arrest to the charges and put you in handcuffs."

"Where are you taking me?"

"Well, since this town's jail got blown down, I'll have to lock you in a room behind Mexican Joe's saloon for tonight. Unless, of course, you'll cooperate and tell me where I can find Link Houston. Tell me that and I might even dismiss all charges against you."

Laura raised her chin. "I don't know anything about any Link Houston."

"Now you're lying to me. You were seen with him here yesterday. That horse you're riding has Ben Houston's brand. Come on. Let's go."

Elijah stepped between them again. "You're not putting my daughter in a room behind that filthy saloon. You're not taking her anywhere."

Smith looked at Elijah for a moment. Then his gloved fist crashed into Elijah's face, knocking him to the ground. Almost before Elijah sprawled to the ground, Smith's gun was in his hand. There was a "click" as he thumbed the hammer back. He leveled the gun at the fallen man.

"No!" Laura screamed. She threw herself between them. "I won't cause you any trouble. I'll go with you."

Smith gave her a hard look. He slowly relaxed and shoved the gun back into his holster.

Almost as an afterthought, he brought his boot down on Elijah's head, grinding his face in the dirt. "Just a reminder not to mess with an officer of the law, Preacher."

Then he led Laura away.

Chapter Nineteen

Smith, with one of his deputies, rode out to Ben Houston's ranch. He saw that the ranch house had been reduced to rubble, but part of the barn was still standing.

Smith and his deputy tied the reins of their horses to a hitching rail. They went into the barn. Ben Houston was there, sorting out some personal belongings he had brought in from the rain.

"Are you Ben Houston?" the sheriff asked.

Ben looked at the two men. Water was dripping from their raincoats. The taller of the two had a sheriff's badge pinned to his shirt pocket.

"I am," Ben replied.

"You got a son named Link?"

Ben nodded.

"Is he here with you?"

A wry smile twisted Ben's lips. "Look around. You don't see him, do you?"

Smith took a step closer. "Don't get mouthy with me. I asked you a question. I expect an answer."

Ben returned his hard look. "No, he's not here. He was killed when the tornado hit the stagecoach last Friday."

"How do you know he was killed?"

"Wasn't everyone on the stage killed?"

"Have you seen his body?"

"I don't think they've found all the bodies yet."

Smith's black eyes were becoming dangerous. "You're lying to me. Link Houston was seen in town yesterday."

"Who saw him?"

"Walt Sawyer. He talked to your son. The preacher's daughter was with him."

Ben snorted. "You believe that drunk? He was probably seeing things."

"I believe him. I don't believe you."

Ben shrugged. "Makes no difference to me."

"Oh, you're wrong about that. It makes a lot of difference. How did you lose your arm?"

"At Gettysburg."

"Johnny Reb, eh?"

Ben nodded.

"I hate Rebs. Killed some of my kin at Shiloh."

"A lot of good men were killed there on both sides."

Smith made a motion to his deputy. The heavy man grabbed Ben. Ben struggled, but with only one arm, he couldn't hold his own against the burly man. He pinned Ben against a wall.

Smith went up to them and hit Ben hard in the stomach. The old soldier doubled over, the breath knocked out of him. The deputy shoved him to the ground. Smith kicked him hard several times in the chest and face. Then he knelt beside Ben, who was gasping for breath.

"How would you like for me to take your other arm off, Johnny Reb? You'd look pretty silly, running around with no arms at all, wouldn't you? Well, that's exactly what I'm going to do if I don't find out where you got your murdering son hid out. Walt Sawyer tells me your boy has a busted leg. He can't be far from here. I want to know where he is."

Ben got some of his breath back, enough to say, "Drop dead, you filthy rattlesnake."

A cold, dangerous smile touched Smith's lips. He nodded to the deputy. They dragged Ben out into the rain. His blood mingled with rivulets of rainwater and soaked into the mud. Smith went back into the barn. When he came back out, a glow could be seen through gaps in the damaged walls. In a matter of minutes, the whole structure was in flames.

"Lie there in the mud and watch what little you got left burn to the ground, Johnny Reb," Smith said. "And I've got a message for your son. I know you got him hid somewhere around here. When you see him, you tell him that I've arrested his girlfriend, the preacher's daughter. I've locked her up in one of the back rooms of Mexican

Joe's place. I'll have a deputy watching her tonight. Won't be anybody in the room but her and the deputy. He's a pretty mean hombre where women are concerned. He'll be all alone there all night, guarding the preacher's daughter. Tell your son to think about that.''

Ben snarled an epithet.

Smith just gave him one of his cold smiles. He and his deputy mounted their horses and rode off through the rain.

Back in town, Smith had a meeting with Sid Milam. ''I don't have your man yet, but I will soon. I've arrested his girlfriend and got her locked up. If Link Houston cares anything about her, he'll be coming to town to try and rescue her. You can get that five-hundred-dollar reward ready. I'll be collecting it before the day is over.''

Chapter Twenty

Link heard the rider coming up the creekbed. He heard the horse's hooves sloshing through the shallow water. He felt a surge of happiness because he was sure it was Laura returning from town. To be on the safe side, he strapped on the holster with the Colt revolver he'd taken off the dead deputy after the storm wrecked the stagecoach. He put his crutches under his arms and limped out of the tent to a spot behind a boulder where he could get a view of the rider. To his surprise, he saw his father.

Ben rode up the incline to the campsite. He slowly dismounted. Link felt a shock. Ben's face was bruised and swollen. He walked like a man in a lot of pain.

"Ben, what's happened to you?"

They went inside the tent, out of the rain. Ben sank down on one of the cots. "Got any whiskey left?"

Link handed him a bottle. Ben took several long swallows. "I didn't have any at home. I had some in the barn, but they burned it down. There's nothing there now."

"What are you talking about, Ben? Who burned the barn down?"

"Smith. Him and one of his deputies came to my place. Gave me a pretty good beating. I'm hurt somewhere inside. I think I've got some busted ribs."

Link swore bitterly. "They were looking for me, right? Just like you figured they would."

Ben nodded. "I didn't tell them where you were, though."

"I'm sorry, Ben. You took that beating on my account."

Ben said, "They've got Laura."

Link turned pale. "What?"

"Smith arrested her. Says he's got her locked up in one of the rooms behind Mexican Joe's saloon."

"Oh, my God," Link whispered. "Ben, you've got to help me hitch up the buckboard."

Ben looked up with swollen, bloodshot eyes. "Don't be a fool, Link. There's nothing you can do."

"Don't tell me there isn't. You don't think I'm going to just sit here? I've got to get Laura away from that man!"

"You wouldn't stand a prairie dog's chance. You don't know what that man's like, Link. He's got pure ice water running in his veins. I've seen men like him before. He's a killing machine. It's his business. He takes pleasure in it.

And he's good at it. He can draw a gun as fast as a rattle-snake strikes. You wouldn't stand a chance going up against him.''

"Ben, I'm not asking your advice. You know I can't ride a horse with my broke leg. I asked if you'd help me hitch up the buckboard. If you won't help, I'll do it myself somehow.''

Ben shrugged. He arose painfully and limped outside. Link tightened the gun belt around his waist, put on a slicker and fitted the crutches under his arms. He went outside, grabbed the buckboard seat and pulled himself up. Ben handed him the reins.

"You're a darn fool, Link. All you'll do is get yourself killed.''

"It really don't make any difference, Ben. Without Laura, I don't care a whole lot about living.''

They looked at each other for a long moment. Then Link slapped the reins on the horse's rump. The wagon began moving. He guided the horse down the incline to the creekbed. The wagon wheels rattled over the graveled creek bottom, sending shards of pain up his broken leg. He was hardly aware of the pain. He was too filled with a different kind of pain.

The winding creekbed took him to Ben's ranch. He saw the smoldering ruins of the barn. Then he was on the main road into Endless.

It was late afternoon when he topped a ridge and started into the town. The rain had slacked a bit to a heavy mist. The clouds, however, had grown darker, more threatening.

He drove past the shack where Fiddling Joe was sitting under a shelter of canvas, sawing away on his fiddle. He paused and waved the bow. "Hello, Link Houston. They're expecting you." Then he went back to fiddling.

Link drove the wagon down to Main Street. When he approached Mexican Joe's saloon, he saw three men on the saloon's front porch, where they were protected from the rain by the porch roof. He stopped the wagon and looked at them through the mist.

The men were sitting on a bench. They stood up. One was taller than the other two. Link saw a badge on his shirt pocket.

Link crawled clumsily from the wagon seat. He reached for the crutches, fitting them under his arms. He turned to face the men on the saloon porch. The mist had become a heavier drizzle. There was a deep, threatening rumble from the dark clouds overhead. From a distance could be heard the wailing sound of the fiddler.

Link called out, "You Sheriff Smith?"

"I am," the tall man said. "And you're Link Houston."

"I came to get Laura Sontag."

"I figured you would."

"You've got no call to lock her up. It's me you want."

"Yes, it is." Smith moved his coat back away from his gun holster. "I want you dead or alive. What's it going to be?"

"How do I know you'll set Laura free without hurting her if I give myself up?"

"Well, we'll have to give that some thought. She did

break the law, helping a fugitive hide. That's called obstructing justice. My deputy, Pete, here, will be disappointed if we just let her go. He was looking forward to spending tonight guarding her.''

The one called Pete, a man with dirty, matted hair, dark beard, and a bearlike body, gave a rumbling chuckle.

''You stinking dog,'' Link said.

Smith's black eyes turned into chips of coal. ''It's not wise to curse me, Houston.'' His hand moved toward his gun.

Link balanced himself with one crutch. He dropped the other, freeing his gun hand. He pushed his slicker back so he could get to his revolver.

Smith drew first.

Before he could shoot, a figure who had been staggering up the boardwalk through the rain, shouted his name in a voice that carried for blocks. ''Smith!''

Momentarily distracted, the sheriff swung his gun in the man's direction.

''I know who you are!'' Elijah Sontag called. His face was bloody. He was clutching his side as if trying to hold the pain in. His eyes were wild. But his voice was strong. It was the powerful, resonant voice that could fill a meeting hall with his sermons. ''Yes, I know you, now. I lost my faith because I thought God brought this terrible tragedy to our town. I blamed him and I cursed him. That's what we do when things go bad. We blame God. But now I know. I figured it out. It ain't God that causes those bad things. It's the forces of evil. It's the devil. You're the devil,

Smith, and the tornado was your messenger. You're not human. You're the devil in human form, and you came to Endless!''

A throbbing vein stood out on Smith's forehead. ''You crazy old fool!'' he shouted, and the gun in his hand blazed. Elijah clutched his chest and fell off the boardwalk.

In that split second, Link fired.

Smith looked startled. He tried to bring his gun hand up, but his revolver had become too heavy. It dropped to the ground. His mouth worked. No sound came out. The fire in his coal-black eyes faded out. He took one stumbling step forward, then sprawled from the porch facedown into the mud.

Both deputies who had stood on either side of him drew their guns. But two shots rang out, coming from behind Link. The force of the .45 slugs threw one of the deputies back against the wall. He dropped his gun and looked open-mouthed down at the blood spurting from his dirty shirt-front. Then he died and slid down the wall to the porch floor. The other deputy had fallen into the mud beside Smith.

Link turned around. He stared at Ben Houston astride his horse, holding his smoking revolver. He was holding the horse's reins in his teeth.

''Ben!'' Link said. ''I didn't know you could shoot like that!''

Ben shoved his revolver back in his holster and took the reins in his hand. ''How the heck do you think I stayed alive through four years of war?''

"I never saw you behind me. I thought you stayed back in camp.''

"Well, I changed my mind. I was some ways behind you, but I caught up when I reached town. You never looked back once or you would have seen me.''

Link picked up his fallen crutch and hobbled to Ben's side. He reached up. Ben clasped his hand.

"Thanks . . . Dad.''

"It's okay, Son.'' Then he said, "It's nice to be on the winning side of a war for a change. Now, come on, let's get Laura out of that stinking room and back into your arms where she belongs.''

When they later told the story of what happened in Endless, Texas, that day, they said there was a brilliant flash of lightning and a clap of thunder when Link fired the bullet that killed Smith. They say the rain stopped shortly after that and the clouds drifted away. At sunset, there was a rainbow stretching across the blue sky over Endless. At least, that's the way the old-timers later told the story.

Epilogue

When the telegraph lines were repaired a few days later, the mayor sent an appeal to Austin, and a Texas Ranger was dispatched to Endless to restore law and order.

Elijah Sontag survived the gunshot wound to his chest. Endless gradually recovered from the tornado. The church members rebuilt the church. Two years after the tornado, very few scars remained from the storm.

Link Houston was given a second trial. Jake Simms testified that he had lied at Link's first trial and that he had bribed Walt on Sid Milam's orders. Simms's testimony forced Walt Sawyer to confess that he'd accepted the bribe. He admitted lying about seeing Link leave the bank building the night of the murder. Actually, it was Sid Milam he'd seen leaving the bank after the shooting. Angelita

Milam signed a deposition that admitted her romance with Albert Milam and told of Sid Milam's violent jealousy.

Walt Sawyer and Jake Simms served brief sentences for their perjury at Link's first trial.

Link was acquitted of the murder charge. He and Laura Sontag were married. By then, Elijah Sontag had recovered enough to administer the vows. Fiddling Joe played the wedding music. He had the only musical instrument in town that hadn't been damaged by the storm.

Ben Houston eventually paid off his note to Sid Milam's bank. However, since all the bank's papers and mortgage notes had blown away in the storm, he took his own sweet time doing it.

Link helped Ben Houston rebuild his house. Then Ben gave him a part of the ranch, where he and Laura built their house. Link eventually became one of the state's most prosperous ranchers.

Sid Milam was charged with the murder of his brother. He pleaded the unwritten law, which was an excellent defense in Texas. Texas juries were inclined to be lenient toward a man who shot his wife's lover. Milam was acquitted. He went on to become a state senator. During his second term, he contracted pneumonia in Austin, and died. His widow, Angelita Milam, regained control of her father's land.

Later, people who wrote about frontier history did extensive research about Endless and the tornado of 1889. They searched diligently for information about the man who called himself "Smith." There were numerous speculations, that he was a gunslinger from Arizona, that he'd been a lawman in Nevada, but the leads all came to a dead end. Nothing about who the man was or where he came from could ever be authenticated and the historians finally gave up. He was just somebody who rode into Endless in the wake of the tornado. . . .